# IL PRIMO LIBRO DE MADRIGALI
# E CANZONI FRANCEZI
# FOR FIVE VOICES

# RECENT RESEARCHES IN THE MUSIC OF THE RENAISSANCE

*James Haar, general editor*

A-R Editions, Inc., publishes seven series of musicological editions
that present music brought to light in the course of current research:

*Recent Researches in the Music of the Middle Ages and Early Renaissance*
Charles M. Atkinson, general editor

*Recent Researches in the Music of the Renaissance*
James Haar, general editor

*Recent Researches in the Music of the Baroque Era*
Christoph Wolff, general editor

*Recent Researches in the Music of the Classical Era*
Eugene K. Wolf, general editor

*Recent Researches in the Music of the Nineteenth and Early Twentieth Centuries*
Rufus Hallmark and D. Kern Holoman, general editors

*Recent Researches in American Music*
H. Wiley Hitchcock, general editor

*Recent Researches in the Oral Traditions of Music*
Philip V. Bohlman, general editor

Each *Recent Researches* edition is devoted to works
by a single composer or to a single genre of composition.
The contents are chosen for their potential interest to scholars
and performers, then prepared for publication according to the
standards that govern the making of all reliable historical editions.

Subscribers to any of these series, as well as patrons of subscribing institutions,
are invited to apply for information about the "Copyright-Sharing Policy"
of A-R Editions, Inc., under which policy any part of an edition
may be reproduced free of charge for study or performance.

Address correspondence to

A-R EDITIONS, INC.
801 Deming Way
Madison, Wisconsin 53717

RECENT RESEARCHES IN THE MUSIC OF THE RENAISSANCE • VOLUME 88

Hubert Waelrant

# IL PRIMO LIBRO DE MADRIGALI E CANZONI FRANCEZI FOR FIVE VOICES

Edited by Gerald R. Hoekstra

 A-R Editions, Inc.
Madison

*Library of Congress Cataloging-in-Publication Data*

Waelrant, Hubert, 1516 or 17–1595.
    [Madrigali e canzoni francezi, 1. libro]
    Il primo libro de madrigali e canzoni francezi : for five voices /
Hubert Waelrant ; edited by Gerald R. Hoekstra.
    1 score. — (Recent researches in the music of the Renaissance,
ISSN 0486-123X ; v. 88)
    For superius, contratenor, quinta, tenor, and bassus.
    Italian and French words, also printed as text with English
translations on p.
    Edited from partbooks (Anvers : H. Waelrant & J. Latio, 1558) in
the Bayerische Staatsbibliothek, Munich.
    Includes bibliographical references.
    ISBN 0-89579-255-9
    1. Madrigals (Music), Italian.   2. Chansons, Polyphonic.
I. Hoekstra, Gerald R.   II. Title.   III. Series.
M2.R2384   vol. 88                  90-754332
[M1582]

# Contents

# Preface

By the mid-sixteenth century the cities of the Low Countries had ceased to be among the leading centers of musical composition in Europe. Most of the great composers born there had sought their musical fortunes elsewhere, in such places as the churches and ducal chapels of Italy, at the imperial Hapsburg court in Austria, or in the Capilla Flamenca of Charles V and his successor, Philip II. Gombert, Arcadelt, and Willaert—among those born around the turn of the century—and Rore, Lassus, and Wert—of the younger generation—were only a few of the important Netherlanders who left their homelands. Yet even after its most prominent sons had left, the Low Countries continued to be important as a musical center. Antwerp, in particular, served as home to a number of musicians in the mid and later sixteenth century; it played an even more important role as a center of music publishing. There the printing establishments of Tielman Susato, Waelrant and Laet, Christophe Plantin, and Phalèse and Bellère issued large numbers of significant collections of music from the 1540s on.

One of the musicians who remained in Antwerp was Hubert Waelrant. His significance and the quality of his music have been pointed out by various scholars,[1] yet almost none of his music is published in modern editions. Most of the scholarly attention given to Waelrant has focused on the motets, which compare favorably with those of contemporaries such as Clemens non Papa, Gombert, and Crecquillon.[2] Even so, few of the motets have been published in modern editions, and none is widely available.[3] His secular partsongs have likewise received far less attention in scholarly literature, although several have appeared in modern prints,[4] among them the popular "Vorria morire" a 4 from *Symphonia angelica*—published earlier with a Flemish text.[5] Thus, the present edition of Waelrant's *Il Primo Libro de Madrigali e Canzoni Francezi* fills a void in our understanding of the work of this talented Netherlander and helps to flesh out our picture of the secular partsong in the Low Countries.

## The Composer

Hubert Waelrant was born in 1516 or 1517 and died in 1595.[6] He appears to have lived and worked in Antwerp his entire life. Fétis stated that he studied in Venice with Adrian Willaert but offered no documentation.[7] Although this claim has been questioned by most scholars, no hard evidence having yet been discovered, it was supported by Lowinsky, who recognized some Venetian style characteristics in Waelrant's motets.[8] Most of our information regarding the composer's life comes from documents in the Antwerp city archives and the Antwerp cathedral archives. These documents refer to three men named Hubert Waelrant who resided in the city during the time; the items that refer to our musician have been sorted out by Walter Piel and Robert Weaver, among others.

Waelrant led a varied musical career as singer, teacher, and music publisher. He served as tenor soloist at the Antwerp cathedral, although for how long it is not known. Cathedral archives document payments made to him in 1544–45 for singing in *het lof*, a daily worship service, and also in several masses. He is referred to again in 1549 as a singer and in 1563 as a composer. The city archives inform us that Waelrant also taught singing at a music school of the Antwerp instrumentalist Gregorius de Coninck in a cooperative arrangement for rental of a house.[9] The contract stipulates that Waelrant would teach singing to de Coninck's pupils without payment in exchange for rent. It seems likely, as Piel suggests, that he taught solfège rather than singing proper. Waelrant, in fact, has been credited with invention of a system of solfège called *bocedization*, or *voces belgicae*. This added a seventh syllable to the traditional hexachord—Waelrant used the syllables *bo-ce-di-ga-lo-me-ni*—and thereby provided an octave series that could be used on either C or F (with B-flat).[10] Other documents inform us that Waelrant served as a consultant for tuning three new bells at the cathedral in 1563; that he was married for the second time in 1568 (his first wife had died); and that he had six children, one of whom, Raymund, became organist in Cologne and, after 1585, at the Antwerp cathedral. Apart from the occasional publication of a new piece, little is known of Waelrant's life from 1558 until his death.

Besides working as a singer, music teacher, and composer, Waelrant collaborated with the Antwerp printer Jan de Laet as music editor and publisher. Their first joint venture, a book of five- and six-voice motets, was issued in 1554. During the next four years the two produced sixteen volumes together. Waelrant selected the musical compositions for the volumes, primarily anthologies of motets and chansons, and Laet attended to the typesetting and printing.[11] The sixteen volumes produced by Waelrant and Laet included a series of eight motet books under the title *Sacrarum Cantionum*—six books *a 5* and *a 6*, and two books *a 4*. The series included over five hundred motets. A four-volume series of chansons and French psalm settings was issued under the title *Jardin musical* in 1555–56.[12] For these anthologies Waelrant chose music primarily by his fellow Netherlanders. Among those selected for inclusion in both series were Clemens non Papa, Thomas Crecquillon, Adrian Tubal, Christian Hollander, and Jean Maillard. Pieces by Waelrant himself also were included in both series, and the sixth book of motets (undated, but published between 1556 and 1558) was devoted entirely to his music. The remaining volumes jointly issued by Waelrant and Laet were three books of French psalm settings by Jean Louys and the book of madrigals and chansons *a 5* to which the present volume is devoted.

We do not know whether the association of Waelrant and Laet continued past 1558, the date of the last work they are known to have published together. The nineteenth-century Belgian musicologist Alphonse Goovaert, thought that their association lasted until Laet's death in 1567, primarily on the basis of a 1565 publication, *Symphonia angelica*, that Goovaerts listed but that probably never existed.[13] Although the output of the two was not large in comparison with that of their contemporaries Susato and Phalèse, the volumes they produced are noteworthy for their fine quality and for the care evidenced in the printing of accidentals and text underlay.

Waelrant's musical output is moderately large and diverse. It numbers twenty-five motets, about half of them in two parts; some thirty secular chansons and nine French psalm settings; and nearly seventy Italian madrigals and *napolitane*. His earliest published pieces were nine chansons included by Phalèse in that publisher's anthologies of four-part chansons of 1552 and 1553.[14] His earliest motets appeared in a volume of the Nuremberg publishers Montanus (= Berg) and Neuber in 1553, the *tomus secundus psalmorum selectorum*.[15] Most of Waelrant's chansons and motets, however, were first published by his own firm. Apart from the madrigals of the 1558 volume, the largest group of his Italian-texted pieces comes to us in a volume entirely devoted to his music, *Le canzon napolitane a quattro voce*, published by Girolamo Scotto in Venice in 1565. How these pieces came to Scotto for printing is not known. Seventeen of the thirty *napolitane* in that volume can also be found in a sixteenth-century manuscript in the Winchester College Library.[16] This manuscript, which bears the dates 1564 and 1566, is thought to have been prepared for Queen Elizabeth I of England and provides some of the earliest evidence of English interest in the Italian madrigal.

Waelrant's compositional productivity seems to have declined greatly after the 1565 volume was issued. Only scattered pieces appeared during his later years, all of them secular partsongs. This may have been due, at least in part, to the unstable social and economic conditions resulting from the religious struggles in the Low Countries during the 1570s and early 1580s. In another capacity, however, Waelrant did make an important contribution to the flowering of interest in the Italian madrigal in the Low Countries toward the end of the century: he edited one of the madrigal anthologies published by Phalèse and Bellère, the *Symphonia angelica* of 1585.[17] Besides madrigals of Ruffo, Ferretti, Marenzio, and other Italians, Waelrant included in this anthology five madrigals of his own, only one of which he had published previously.[18]

A number of scholars have seen evidence of Protestant leanings in works by Waelrant. They have noted, for instance, the composer's settings of Marot's metrical psalms, which were associated with the Reformed faith in the Low Countries, and his printing of the three volumes of Louys's psalm versifications. However, while psalm singing was cultivated particularly by Protestants, it was not officially opposed by Catholic authorities in the Low Countries until the early 1560s.[19] Some point to Waelrant's choice of motet texts as further evidence of Protestant sympathies. He left no masses or settings of the Marian texts so popular with his contemporaries. Instead he drew primarily on the Gospels, particularly passages that focus on the life of Christ, his miracles and teachings, and didactic passages that emphasize obedience, love, and humility. Lowinsky thought that the texts suggested affiliation with Anabaptist groups, but Weaver, after an exhaustive study of the subject, concluded that Waelrant cannot be linked firmly with any specific group. He pointed out that the topics of the motet texts resemble those found in the writings of Erasmus of Rotterdam and sixteenth-century Spiritualist groups in the Netherlands as much as those of the Anabaptists.[20]

## The Source

The volume of madrigals and chansons constituting the present edition carries both Italian and French titles. Its title page, reproduced in plate 1, reads:

Di Huberto Waelrant Il Primo Libro de Madrigali & Canzoni Francezi A cinque voci. De Hubert Waelrant Le Primier Livre de Chansons Francoyses & Italianes a cinq voix. [Table of contents] En Anvers. Per Hubert Waelrant & Ioan Latio. Anno. D.CCCCC.LVIII. Avec Previlegie.[21]

The work was printed in five partbooks of thirty-two pages each in quarto format. It is the last known collaborative publication of Waelrant and Laet. Copies of the complete set of partbooks can be found in the Universitetsbiblioteket, Uppsala, and in the Bayerische Staatsbibliothek, Munich. Incomplete copies are held by the British Library, London, and the Universitätsbibliothek, Tübingen.

This publication marks a change in Waelrant's musical output. Its contents include eleven chansons, one of them in two parts, and nine Italian madrigals, all in two parts.[22] The chansons mark a shift to the thicker texture of five voices in his output in that genre. All his previous chansons had been for three or four voices, except for one chanson for six. More significant, however, are the madrigals, which were not only Waelrant's first settings of Italian texts but, in fact, some of the earliest madrigals published in the Low Countries; they were preceded only by those of Lassus's "Opus 1," a volume that contained madrigals and *villanesche* as well as motets and chansons. That had come out only three years earlier.[23] In fact, Waelrant's volume preceded the period of real interest in the madrigal in the Low Countries by more than twenty years. Several other Netherlandish composers published collections containing madrigals during the next decade—Séverin Cornet his *Canzoni napolitane a 4* (1563), Noël Faignient his *Chansons, madrigales, et motetz à 4–6* (1568), and Jean de Castro his *Il primo libro di madrigali, canzoni & motetti a 3* (1569)— but the madrigal seems to have caught on particularly in the 1580s with the issuance of Phalèse and Bellère's popular series of madrigal anthologies.[24]

Waelrant's volume is dedicated to a Bartholomeo Doria Inurea, of whom nothing is known except what can be gleaned from the dedication itself. Among other things, he was a student of the composer; Waelrant refers to himself as Inurea's "loving and grateful teacher." We also learn that Inurea enjoyed discussing music as a diversion from his "daily honorable affairs." Most likely he was a musically talented merchant or banker residing in Antwerp at the time. The dedication reads:

To the Very Magnificent Sir Bartholomeo Doria Inurea:
  Seeing that you (my most honored sir), among your fine and most noble attributes, which like bright stars shine in you, have for some long time been devoted to music, the harmony of which, in the intervals of your daily honorable affairs, you are wont most often to discuss with most merry conversation, I have found nothing more suited to this, your virtuous and honorable delectation, and to the duty of a loving and grateful teacher, than to present you with a part of my compositions, which I occasionally like to practice for my own diversion and for the satisfaction of many of my betters and lords (among whom you are the foremost) rather than for any other reason. Judging that since you love this musical talent ardently and for the fact that I dedicate to you my labor and the fruits thereof, it should be not only welcomed and appreciated with a glad spirit by

you, but also that under the shadow of your name and stature it should remain protected and defended against any malign opposition, certain and sure that under you it will be adorned with those beautiful garments (which the poverty of my talent has never been able to gain for it), you will therefore accept this, my feeble gift, as an earnest of the great sum that I owe you and that your merits deserve, not leaving off loving me nor keeping me under your protection, expecting from me, when it shall be granted me by God above, a still greater and brighter pledge of my affection and regard for you. May God grant you a long and healthy life. Your humble servant,

Hubert Waelrant[25]

Throughout most of the volume, settings of Italian texts alternate with settings of French ones. This pattern is interrupted only with numbers 5 and 6, where two Italian pieces follow in succession; numbers 15 and 16, both French; and numbers 18–20, all French.[26] The other, and musically more important, controlling factor in the organization of the volume is the grouping according to tonal type—that is, by ambitus (as indicated by clef usage), signature, and final—as shown in table 1.[27]

TABLE 1
Modal Organization of Waelrant's *Il Primo Libro*

| Piece | Clefs[a] | Signature | Final | Mode | Language |
|---|---|---|---|---|---|
| 1 | High | ♭ | G | 1 | Italian |
| 2 | High | ♭ | G | 1 | French |
| 3 | High | ♭ | G | 1 | Italian |
| 4 | High | ♭ | F | 5 | French |
| 5 | High | ♭ | F | 5 | Italian |
| 6 | High | ♭ | F | 5 | Italian |
| 7 | Standard | ♮ | G | 8 | French |
| 8 | Standard | ♮ | G | 8 | Italian |
| 9 | Standard | ♮ | G | 8 | French |
| 10 | Standard | ♮ | C | 7? | Italian |
| 11 | Standard | ♮ | E | 3 | French |
| 12 | Standard | ♮ | E | 3 | Italian |
| 13 | Standard | ♭ | G | 2 | French |
| 14 | Standard | ♭ | G | 2 | Italian |
| 15 | Standard | ♭ | G | 2 | French |
| 16 | Standard | ♭ | F | 6 | French |
| 17 | Standard | ♭ | F | 6 | Italian |
| 18 | Standard | ♭ | F | 6 | French |
| 19 | High | ♮ | C | 8? | French |
| 20 | High | ♮ | C | 8? | French |

[a] High (=chiavette): G2, C2, C3, C3, F3
Standard: C1, C3, C4, C4, F4

It will be noted that, except for the "surplus" chansons placed at the end, Waelrant's pattern of alternating chansons and madrigals is broken only where necessitated by the grouping according to tonal type, which took priority. Organizing a volume by tonal type was a common procedure in the mid-sixteenth century. Waelrant and Laet followed this procedure in the volumes of their *Jardin musical* series as well.[28]

## Texts: Subjects and Attributions

Although the texts Waelrant chose deal primarily with the vicissitudes of love, as one would expect, they show a wide diversity of subjects. Among the French chansons a number are plaints of the languishing and unrequited lover such as occur commonly in medieval and Renaissance chansons. "Dictes ouy ma dame ma maistresse" (no. 7), "Si je maintiens ma vie seulement" (no. 11), and "Or suis je bien au pire" (no. 15) typify the traditional courtly love chanson. Another poem, "D'amours me va tout au rebours" (no. 9), more specifically laments the misfortunes in the life of the lover, for whom everything seems to "go contrary." Two of the chanson poems, both by Clément Marot, employ the theme of May as a month for lovers, but in different and unusual ways: in "Moys amoureux, moys vestu de verdure" (no. 2) the poet denies the power of spring to make him happy unless it also makes his lover happy, and in "Souvent au joly moys de May" (no. 13) he appeals to the fact of his faithfulness even in spring, when others are enticed by new loves, as proof of his constancy.

The remaining chanson texts lie outside the tradition of courtly love poety. "Une pastorelle gentille" (no. 4)—Marot's "Du jour de Noël"—is a rather unusual Christmas song. It starts out like a typical chanson about a shepherd and shepherdess in the greenwood but in the second strophe, surprisingly, turns into a reminder of Christ's birth. Other than this piece, the only religious text is "De tout mon coeur t'exalteray" (no. 18), Marot's versification of Psalm 9, verse 1.[29] As noted earlier, this is one of nine French psalms set by the composer. "De tout mon coeur j'ayme la Marguerite" (no. 19) is one of a number of sixteenth-century settings of poems addressed to "la Marguerite" that laud the nobility, worth, and beauty of the flower (i.e., daisy) as well as, one assumes, a lady of that name.[30] The two remaining French texts are humorous chansons: "Un jour passé bien escoutoye" (no. 16), an amusing song about a young girl's view of the advantages of marriage, and "Soyons playsantz encore demiheure" (no. 20), a French *carpe diem.*

Authors or sources for most of the French texts can be identified. Five of the eleven chanson texts are the work of Clément Marot. The psalm, the noël (Marot's Chanson 25), and the two May poems have already been mentioned. Of the last, "Moys amoureux, moys vestu de verdure" (no. 2) is the poet's "Du moys de May et de Anne" (Epigramme 147), and "Souvent au

joly moys de May" (no. 13) is his "Chant de May et de vertu" (Ballade 19) with the opening line altered.[31] The fifth Marot poem in the volume is the rondeau "D'amours me va tout au rebours" (no. 9; Marot's Chanson 27). The prominence of Marot in this volume is not surprising. The grace, beauty, wit, and simplicity of Marot's poetry made him a favorite among sixteenth-century musicians second only to Ronsard, whose popularity was just beginning to rise in the 1550s.

The author of only one of the remaining chanson texts is known: "Dictes ouy ma dame ma maistresse" (no. 7), which appears anonymously in several manuscripts, is the work of the French king François I.[32] The tribute to the Marguerite, "De tout mon coeur j'ayme la Marguerite" (no. 19), is credited to the *rhétoriqueur* Guillaume Crétin (d. 1525) by Wolfgang Boetticher in his work on Lassus, but that is an error; the poem is anonymous.[33] The remaining four chanson texts are also anonymous. Three of them were printed earlier in anthologies of chanson verse: "Or suis je bien au pire" (no. 15) in *S'ensuyvent plusiers belles chansons nouvelles* (Paris, 1535);[34] "Si je maintiens ma vie seulement" (no. 11) in *Hecatomphile . . . Les Fleurs de poesie francoyse* (Paris, 1534); and "Un jour passé bein escoutoye" (no. 16) in *La Fleur de poesie francoise* (Paris, 1543) as "Aultre [chanson] d'une jeune fiancee estant aux estuves."[35] The source of the poem "Soyons playsantz encore demiheure" (no. 20) is not known.

The Italian texts are more varied than the French, and their content cannot be so easily characterized and summarized, though a number of them deal either directly or indirectly with love. Five of the nine madrigals are settings of poems from Petrarch's *Rime sparse,* or *Canzoniere,* the poet's monumental collection of sonnets and canzone immortalizing his beloved Laura. The prominence of Petrarch in Waelrant's collection is not surprising, considering the general popularity of that poet with madrigalists of this period and particularly with Lassus in his early madrigal collections. The *Rime sparse,* which Petrarch worked on over a period of forty years, consists of two parts, generally referred to as the poems *in vita* (nos. 1–263) and those *in morte* (nos. 264–366).[36] By Petrarch's own account, Laura died of the Black Death in 1348,[37] but he continued to write poems to her and about her. According to Robert Durling, "Laura's death . . . frees his fantasies all the more."[38] Of the five sonnets selected by Waelrant, only one, "Amor piangev' e io con luy tal volta" (no. 5; Petrarch's no. 25), comes from the first group. In it the poet gives thanks for a change of heart in his lover. The other four come from the second part—that is, they were written after Laura's death. In "Sento l'aura mi' antica, e i dolci colli" (no. 3; Petrarch's no.

320), a vision of the hills where he first met his beloved ("l'aura" is, of course, a play on "Laura")[39] brings the poet sorrow from which he finds no repose. In "E mi par d'hor in hor' udir' il messo" (no. 1; Petrarch's no. 349), the poet, having a vision in which he hears a messenger from his departed lover calling to him, laments the misfortunes of his life and longs for the day he can leave his "earthly prison" and join his Lord and his lady in heaven. His yearning for death is given even stronger expression in "Ogni giorno mi par più di mill'anni" (no. 6; Petrarch's no. 357). Here the poet longs to follow his "dear guide [presumably Christ] who led me in the world and now leads me by a better way to a life without troubles." The light of his vision shines so strongly in his heart that he is counting days. The "King" of the sestet, who suffered "threats of death" with "worse pain," refers, of course, to Christ also. "Volo con l'ali di pensier' al cielo" (no. 17; Petrarch's no. 362) speaks of visions that bring him to heaven and in which he sees his beloved and his Lord. Alas, he is not allowed to stay but is reminded that twenty or thirty years is not too long to wait.

The authors of three of the remaining four madrigal texts can be identified: "Questa fera gentil che scherz' e fugge" (no. 8) is by A. F. Ricc'eri, "Chius'er' il sol d'un tenebroso velo" (no. 10) by Ariosto, and "Ahi dispietat' amor come consenti" (no. 12) by Bernardo Tasso.[40] The sonnet of Ariosto, "Chius'er' il sol," is one of a relatively small number of poems in that form by a poet better known for his epic poetry. It describes a vision of his lover not unlike the visions of Petrarch. Tasso's equally Petrarchan "Ahi dispietat' amor" is the only Italian poem set here that is not a sonnet; it consists of two stanzas in *ottava rima* from the poet's *lontananza* series. In fact, these particular strophes are from a cycle of fifteen *stanze di lontananza* completed in 1544 while the poet was in Antwerp. The *stanze di lontananza*, written to or about his wife, Porzia, were extremely popular with musicians and were intended to be set to music.[41] While "Chius'er' il sol" and "Ahi dispietat' amor," with their serious character, elaborate conceits, classical allusions, and somewhat mysterious meanings, are fairly typical of madrigal poetry, "Questa fera gentil" is less so. It sings the praises of a lissome and charming nymph and concludes with a line more characteristic of the French chanson than the Italian madrigal. The only Italian text whose authorship remains unknown is "Ferma speranz' e fe pur' e sincera" (no. 14). Waelrant's is the only known setting of this poem. The cryptic references to colors and to "il vag' e bel morato" ("the charming, handsome Moor") in the sestet make it an unlikely poem for a composer to select merely for poetic qualities. The colors and the *morato* image may well refer to the heraldic colors and sym-

bol of a family coat of arms. It seems likely that the setting of such a text would have been commissioned, perhaps by the poet.

## The Music

The presence of Lassus in Antwerp in 1555 and the publication of his madrigals there were probably instrumental in inspiring Waelrant to attempt some Italian songs of his own. Indeed, Waelrant's style of madrigal writing resembles that of Lassus and the Romans more than that of the Venetians. Although the exact length of Lassus's stay in Antwerp is not known—he was there for perhaps a year between 1554 and 1556[42]—Waelrant would undoubtedly have known him. His colleague, Jan de Laet, published Lassus's first book of motets in 1556. Waelrant's name does not appear on the title page, even though he and Laet were collaborating on musical publications during this period; Lassus probably oversaw the musical editing of the volume himself. Besides the four-part madrigals published by Susato, Waelrant probably would have encountered Lassus's early five-part madrigals as well, the first book of which was printed by Gardano in Venice in 1555. These, as well as the five-part madrigals included in Antonio Barré's Roman anthologies of the late 1550s, probably date from Lassus's years in Rome.

In settings of his Italian texts, Waelrant combines aspects of the Netherlandish contrapuntal technique with the newer declamatory rhythms and richer harmonies of the madrigal. The texture of his madrigals is fairly dense and usually involves all five voices, but Waelrant frequently drops a voice or two from a phrase to lighten the texture and alter the vocal color. This technique is particularly effective when phrases are repeated with a different voicing. Waelrant employs a variety of textures within a given piece, shifting from one phrase to the next between strict and loosely chordal textures, between imitative and free contrapuntal writing. Although occasionally he employs a strict point of imitation at the beginning of a madrigal (see, e.g., nos. 6 and 17), more frequently he writes merely rhythmic imitation or incorporates free voices within an otherwise imitative context (cf. nos. 1, 8, and 14). Occasionally he opens with a declamatory chordal passage (nos. 5 and 12). Internal phrases are just as varied, though the prevailing textures are modified homophony and free counterpoint.

The richness of Waelrant's harmonies and the frequency of chromatic alterations in the madrigals show that the composer perceived these as key elements of the madrigal style. While his harmonies are rarely jarring—he uses flats only on E and B, sharps only on F, C, and G—they introduce subtle shifts of tonal focus that draw the listener's attention. In fact, in some of the madrigals Waelrant introduces a harmonic surprise as early as the opening phrase. In "Sento l'aura mi' antica, e i dolci colli" (no. 3), for example, a cross relation occurs between the two highest voices at the first barline; and in "Amor piangev' e io con luy tal volta" (no. 5), after F has been established as the focus of the opening four measures, the harmony shifts surprisingly to an E-flat chord in measure 5. Often these harmonic shifts serve expressive purposes. This is particularly true when the composer underscores words expressing sweetness, sadness, pain, or grief, or words referring to death, with a move to "flat harmonies" (chords with B-flat or E-flat as either root or third). This was a convention commonly used by composers in the midsixteenth century, including Lassus. In setting the words "con più grave pena" ("with worse pain") in the *seconda parte* of "Ogni giorno mi par più di mill' anni" (no. 6), for instance, Waelrant introduces G minor and B-flat major harmonies and moves on the repetition of the phrase to E-flat harmonies. Noteworthy here also is the diminished E-flat harmony preceding the cadence at measures 13–14. (In addition to the chromatic harmonies of the setting of "con più grave pena," Waelrant also uses broader rhythmic movement and drawn-out suspensions to underscore this phrase.) Waelrant's chromaticism sometimes clearly serves expressive purposes and sometimes does not. In the *prima parte* of the same madrigal, the rich chromatic harmonies of measures 19–23 suggest "gl'inganni del mondo" ("the deceits of the world") mentioned in the text, though the equally chromatic setting of "et hor novellament' in ogni vena" ("and which recently [entered] each vein") in the *seconda parte* serves no obvious expressive purpose.

One of the most significant aspects of the midsixteenth-century madrigal, of course, is the relation between text and music. While Waelrant seems more interested in expressive text painting of the sort mentioned above, he occasionally employs pictorial conventions as well. The opening line of "Volo con l'ali di pensier' al cielo" (no. 17) ("I fly with the wings of thought to heaven"), for example, he sets with a rising melodic line that reaches its apogee in each voice on the word "cielo." But such instances are rare.

Waelrant also evinces a familiarity with that other important dimension of text setting in madrigals, declamation. While he does not always follow textual accentuation strictly in setting the words, he does usually emphasize important syllables with longer note values, melodic leaps, or placement on the tactus.

Frequently Waelrant's rhythms suggest the sort of free declamatory writing associated with the *madrigale*

*arioso* but found in works by Lassus as well. Usually these rhythms are inspired by the textual accents, as in the setting of "nel qual io viv' e morto giacer volli" at the end of the *prima parte* of "Sento l'aura mi' antica, e i dolci colli" (no. 3). Such rhythms, however, are equally frequent in the chansons (cf. "Moys amoureux, moys vestu de verdure" [no. 2], mm. 10–13). In both genres, but in the madrigals especially, rhythms vary greatly from one phrase to the next. Indeed, the variety of rhythmic movement in Waelrant's madrigals seems even greater than that in Lassus's five-part madrigals. Phrases in the broader rhythms of breves and semibreves are followed abruptly by phrases set with lively rhythmic semiminims. These semiminim patter rhythms frequently involve pairs of notes on the same pitch and are usually loosely contrapuntal rather than homorhythmic. Waelrant seems to like these lively rhythms; indeed, in some madrigals they predominate (cf., e.g., "E mi par d'hor in hor' udir' il messo" [no. 1]). One thinks of such patter rhythms as being more characteristic of the sixteenth-century chanson than the madrigal; they are, however, not uncommon in the *madrigale a note nere* (or black-note madrigal) and the *madrigale arioso*. (It is worth noting, though, that Waelrant uses the ₵ mensuration sign here rather the C of the black-note madrigal.) Another rhythmic pattern typical of the *madrigale a note nere* is the syncopation of a string of minims. In measure 37 of the *seconda parte* of "Ahi dispietat' amor come consenti" (no. 12), the phrase "mentr'havra verd'allor' e rami" is set in the contratenor to minims that start off the beat. Along with this, one hears the superius and bassus on the same words but with notes on the beat.

The eleven French chansons of *Il Primo Libro* vary in style from piece to piece, depending on the character of the texts. Those with a more serious text, such as "Moys amoureux, moys vestu de verdure" (no. 2) or "Dictes ouy ma dame ma maistresse" (no. 7), show the same variety of rhythms and textures as the madrigals. Even some of the declamatory and expressive devices of the madrigals are present in some chansons. For instance, the phrase "que de tumber in facheuse tristesse" ("than to fall into distressing sorrow") in "Dictes ouy ma dame" is set with the same broad rhythms and movement to flat harmonies one would encounter in a madrigal for a phrase of this character. Likewise, the concern with declamation seen in the madrigals is evidenced in the chansons as well. Generally, however, even the most serious chansons do not show the harmonic richness of the madrigals.

Chansons with less serious texts, on the other hand, generally lack the expressive devices of the madrigals. The Christmas song of Marot, "Une pastorelle gentille" (no. 4), for instance, is quite simple harmonically and has lively rhythms throughout. Only the reference to the Virgin ("la belle Pucelle") does Waelrant set off with slower movement and E-flat major harmonies. For the more amusing texts of "Un jour passé bien escoutoye" (no. 16) and "Soyons playsantz encore demiheure" (no. 20), he uses lively rhythms and more chordal writing. The psalm versification "De tout mon coeur t'exalteray" (no. 18) fittingly receives a more staid treatment.

Even the most madrigal-like of the chansons, however, are distinguished by certain traditional characteristics of chanson style. Short rhythmic units, frequently repeated and often without harmonic changes, contribute a vivacity to the chansons generally lacking in the madrigals. These short motives, usually of four notes, evolve directly from the chanson's poetic line. French verse of this time typically consists of octosyllabic or decasyllabic lines with a caesura after the fourth syllable (4 + 4 or 4 + 6). It is the opening four-syllable hemistich that is usually set with a short four-note motive. The caesura is often accompanied by a break in the musical line, and frequently the hemistich is repeated. For example, in "Moys amoureux, moys vestu de verdure" (no. 2), the opening two words are repeated in each voice and followed by a rest before the remainder of the line is sung. Frequently the short hemistichs are sung to semiminims (cf. the settings of "fais seulement" and "incontinent" in the same chanson) and may be repeated several times, creating the lively rhythms and short phrase units. While madrigal verse also has caesuras, the hemistichs are generally slightly longer. Furthermore, Waelrant tends more often to set his madrigal lines complete.

Another manifestation of traditional chanson style that distinguishes these works from the madrigals of the volume is the presence of the characteristic rhythm o ♩♩ or ♩ ♪♪. While the madrigals begin with a great variety of rhythms, all but two of the chansons (4 and 19) open with this pattern. The variation typical for internal phrases, ⌐ ♩♩♩, is equally common.

Waelrant's *Il Primo Libro*, with its alternation of chansons and madrigals, offers the modern scholar an interesting opportunity to examine the two principal genres of sixteenth-century secular song as understood by a Netherlander working in the 1550s. Waelrant's skill in writing in both genres is evident throughout the volume, in the chansons as well as the madrigals. That he understood the subtleties of madrigal writing seems especially noteworthy, since he was one of the first northerners to write in the new genre.

## Editorial Procedures

This edition of Waelrant's *Il Primo Libro de Madrigali e Canzoni Francezi* is based on the complete set of part-books in the Bayerische Staatsbibliothek, Munich. The incipit preceding each piece gives the mensuration sign, clef, and first note of each part as it appears in the source. I have indicated the range of each voice immediately before the modern clef. In place of the variety of clefs in the source, this edition employs only three: treble, tenor G-clef, and bass. Titles, present in the source only in a table of contents, are added here to the music pages and are extended to include the entire first line to make identification of texts easier. The numbering of the pieces is editorial and treats multiple *parti* of a composition as a single piece. The order of the pieces is that of the source.

Note values of the source have been retained in this edition, except for final longas, which appear here as breves under fermatas. I have added barlines to facilitate reading and study, but they should not be interpreted as having any bearing on the rhythm. Ligatures are found only rarely in the source, and I have designated them here in the usual way with solid horizontal brackets ( ⌐—⌐ ).

In the source for this edition, as in most sixteenth-century prints, accidentals generally apply only to the note that follows and successive notes of the same pitch. They are usually canceled by movement to another pitch, particularly if it is a minim or greater note value. A common exception occurs in the ornamental figure found with many suspensions, especially at cadences, in which the inflected pitch moves to its lower neighbor before returning to the note of resolution. Here the accidental precedes the ornament, but it clearly applies to the note of resolution as well. Whether a rest cancels an accidental is not as clear; when neither the harmony nor the voicing changes, it seems likely that the inflection would be retained.

In this edition all accidentals found in the source are printed on the staff, even those rendered redundant in modern notational practice. This enables performers and readers to reconstruct the original print without consulting the Preface. Accidentals printed above the staff are editorial, either as cautionary accidentals or musica ficta.

As editor I encountered no great problems with text underlay. In all of their publications Waelrant and Laet aligned words and notes with great care. Furthermore, the settings of the present volume are largely syllabic, making text underlay obvious. Textual repetitions are usually indicated with *ij* in the source. Occasionally this sign is missing and there is merely a blank space, but it is clear that text is to be repeated. In a few instances only the beginning of a repeated line of text is printed and its remainder indicated with the sign "&c." Textual repetitions indicated in any of these ways in the source are written out and placed in angle brackets.

For the most part spelling and capitalization follow

the source. I have made two general alterations, however: I have written out all abbreviations, including ampersands, and have changed *u, v,* and *i* to *v, u,* and *j* where appropriate, following modern printing conventions. Otherwise I have not modernized the spellings, though I have made other changes for the sake of consistency. Neither French nor Italian orthography had been standardized yet at this time, and therefore it is not surprising that the texts in the source show frequent inconsistencies in spelling. Often a word appears with different spellings within a single passage, usually between different voices but occasionally within the same voice.[43] The greater frequency of errors and inconsistencies in the Italian texts suggests that the typesetter, and perhaps Waelrant himself, had a poorer grasp of Italian than French. In most cases I have adopted the spelling that appears in the majority of the parts for all of them. Occasionally three parts have an erroneous rather than variant reading, and in such cases I have adopted the correct rather than majority reading. I have followed the source for contractions and elisions also, except where it is inconsistent; in such cases I have regularized by choosing one of the possibilities offered. In certain cases apostrophes have been inserted where they were absent but necessary. I have also added accents where they are lacking in the source, either by mistake or because accentuation was no more standard than other aspects of spelling at this time. Where authoritative editions of the poetry are available, as in the cases of Marot, Petrarch, Ariosto, and François I, I have consulted them, but I have allowed contractions and acceptable alternate spellings to stand.

Since there is no punctuation of the texts in the source, all punctuation here is editorial. Where authoritative modern editions of the poetry exist, I have usually adopted the punctuation in them. Otherwise, the punctuation is my own.

Most authorities agree that, in spite of the different spellings, sixteenth-century pronunciation did not differ substantially from modern pronunciation, even for the French.[44] Where an obsolete *s* appears in French words, as in *maistresse* (*maîtresse*), it should not be pronounced. In these cases orthography had not yet caught up with pronunciation, and the words should be pronounced as they are today.

## Critical Notes

Other than the inconsistencies of spelling and punctuation mentioned above, few problems faced the editor in preparing this edition. The music was largely free from errors. The following list notes minor errors in the source or deviations from the source in this edition.

[5] *Amor piangev' e io con luy tal volta*
   *Seconda parte*
   M. 37, Quinta: note 5 is missing in the source.

[6] *Ogni giorno mi par più di mill'anni*
   M. 3, Superius: note 1 has a ♯ (i.e., natural), creating an augmented octave with the bass.

[8] *Questa fera gentil che scherz' e fugge*
   *Seconda parte*
   M. 36, Tenor: note 2 has a cautionary ♯.

[13] *Souvent au joly moys de May*
   M. 24, Contratenor: note 2 has a ♯

[14] *Ferma speranz' e fe pur' e sincera*
   Mm. 27–28, Superius: read "E in me *per* temp' " for "E in me temp'." M. 28, Superius: note 2 replaces two eighth notes of the same pitch. M. 35, Quinta: note 2 has a ♯.

[15] *Or suis je bien au pire*
   M. 16, beats 3–4: although this is an unusual chord for the time, there is no obvious melodic correction that would yield preferable harmony.

## Acknowledgments

I am grateful to the Bayerische Staatsbibliothek, Munich, for supplying the microfilm copy of Waelrant's *Il Primo Libro de Madrigali e Canzoni Francezi* and granting permission to prepare this edition of it; to Saint Olaf College for providing a Summer Study Grant that enabled me to do much of the work for this edition; and to Robert Durling and Harvard University Press for allowing me to use Professor Durling's translations of Petrarch. A special thanks to two colleagues from the college across town, Professors Charles Messner and Cathy Yandell of Carleton College. Professor Messner provided translations of the dedication and four madrigal texts. Professor Yandell gave generously of her time and expertise in early French to provide valuable criticism regarding my translations of the chanson texts. Finally, I would like to express my appreciation to Christopher Hill of A-R Editions for his many helpful suggestions and for his careful attention to detail, both of which have made this a better volume than it would otherwise have been.

# Notes

1. Nanie Bridgman notes that "a study of his works shows him to have been a musician with a great love of novelty who has hitherto been unjustly neglected." See "Sacred Music on the Continent: The Franco-Flemings in the North," *New Oxford History of Music*, vol. 4 (London: Oxford University Press, 1968), 235. Edward Lowinsky, *Secret Chromatic Art in the Netherlands Motet*, trans. Carl Buchman (New York: Columbia University Press, 1946), and Robert Lee Weaver, "The Motets of Hubert Waelrant," 2 vols. (Ph.D. diss., Syracuse University, 1971), both draw attention to the imaginative treatment of texts in the motets.

2. The primary scholarly works dealing with Waelrant's motets are Lowinsky, *Secret Chromatic Art*, Weaver, "The Motets," and Walter Piel, *Studien zum Leben und Schaffen Hubert Waelrants unter besonderer Berücksichtigung seiner Motetten*, Marburger Beiträge zur Musikforschung, vol. 3 (Marburg: Gorich & Weiershaüer, 1969).

3. Seven motets are included in Piel, *Studien zum Leben und Schaffen*. All of the motets and three of the French psalms can be found, respectively, in Weaver, "The Motets of Hubert Waelrant," and Howard Slenk, "The Huguenot Psalter in the Low Countries: A Study of Its Monophonic and Polyphonic Manifestations in the Sixteenth Century" (Ph.D. diss., The Ohio State University, 1965).

4. One villanella appears in Godelieve Spiessens, ed., *Luitmuziek van Emanuel Adriaenssen*, Monumenta Musicae Belgicae, vol. 10 (Berchem-Antwerp: "De Ring," 1966), and another (with Flemish text) in Fritz Noske, "Remarques sur les luthistes des Pays-Bas (1580–1620)," in *Le Luth et sa musique*, ed. Jean Jacquot (Paris: Centre national de la recherche scientifique, 1958). A chanson, "Musiciens qui chantez," appears in both William Barclay Squire, *Ausgewählte Madrigale und mehrstimmige Gesänge berühmter Meister des 16., 17. Jahrhunderts* (Leipzig: Breitkopf & Härtel, n.d.), and Albert Lavignac, ed., *Encyclopédie de la musique et dictionnaire du Conservatoire*, pt. 1, vol. 3 (Paris: C. Delagrave, 1915), 1825–29. Another chanson, "D'amours me va tout au rebours" from *Il Primo Libro*, was printed recently in *The Oxford Book of French Chansons*, ed. Frank Dobbins (Oxford: Oxford University Press, 1987). Other individual pieces appear in various nineteenth-century publications.

5. "Als ik u vinde," in Emanuel Adriaenssen's *Pratum Musicum* (Antwerp, 1584); modern edition in Noske, "Remarques sur les luthistes des Pays-Bas." *Symphonia angelica di diversi excellentissimi musici* was published in 1585. Waelrant set the text of "Vorria morire" three times: twice for four voices and once for six. Weaver is incorrect in treating the four-voice settings of the Winchester manuscript (his catalogue, no. 54) and *Symphonia angelica* as the same piece (cf. Weaver, "The Motets," 2:114). These are two different settings. It was the setting from *Symphonia angelica* (and *Pratum Musicum*) that appeared frequently in later collections of partsongs, often with substitute texts.

6. Franciscus Sweertius, *Athenae Belgicae* (Antwerp, 1628), states that the composer died on 19 November 1595 at the age of 78. Thus, he would have been born (or bap-

tized) between 20 November 1516 and 19 November 1517. For a thorough review of the literature and documentation concerning Waelrant's life, see Piel, *Studien zum Leben und Schaffen*, and Weaver, "The Motets."

7. François-Joseph Fétis, *Biographie universelle des musiciens*, 2d ed., 8 vols. (Paris: Firmin-Didot, 1866–70), 8:392.

8. Lowinsky, *Secret Chromatic Art*, 70 n. 97. See also p. 88, where the author suggests that Waelrant and Laet's printing techniques are modeled after those of Gardano in Venice.

9. See Howard Slenk, "The Music School of Hubert Waelrant," *Journal of the American Musicological Society* 21 (1968): 157–67.

10. The claim that Waelrant invented *bocedization* goes back to Sweertius, the early seventeenth-century musician and biographer who claimed to have been Waelrant's pupil. It should be noted, however, that another seventeenth-century writer, Johann Heinrich Alsted, attributed it to David Mostart (ca. 1560–1615), also a Netherlander. Cf. Piel, *Studien zum Leben und Schaffen*, 39. See also *The New Grove Dictionary of Music and Musicians*, s.v. "Bocedization." Alsted, in his article "Musica" in the *Encyclopaedia VII Tomis Distincta*, cites a treatise of Mostart's that is now lost. Seth Calvisius was an enthusiastic advocate of *bocedization* and argued for its use in several of his treatises.

11. Waelrant describes his part in the collaboration in the prefaces to the first book of motets *a 4* and to book 1 of *Jardin musical à 4*. Laet also published music volumes under his own name alone, including works by Lassus, Cornet, Faignient, and Jean de Castro. As Weaver, "The Motets" 1:30 n. 49, notes, the 1556 publication of Lassus motets bears the name of Laet only, not Waelrant and Laet, as claimed erroneously by Lowinsky, *Das antwerpener Motettenbuch Orlando di Lasso's* (The Hague: Martinus Nijhoff, 1937), 6, and repeated by Reese and Slenk.

12. The four volumes of *Jardin musical* are published as vols. 29 and 30 of the series The Sixteenth Century Chanson, ed. Jane Bernstein (New York: Garland, 1990).

13. Cf. Weaver, "The Motets," 1:31, and Alphonse Goovaerts, *Histoire et bibliographie de la typographie musicale dans les Pays-Bas* (Antwerp: P. Kockx, 1880), 42 and 232–33. Slenk, "The Music School of Hubert Waelrant," 164, thinks that the association had "apparently been dissolved [by 1563], for in that year Jan de Laet alone published a volume of Cornet's *canzoni napolitane*." However, since Laet also produced alone the 1556 volume of Lassus motets, this does not by itself confirm that the two no longer worked together.

14. Books 2–4 *a 4* (*RISM* 1552[12–14]); book 1 *a 5* and 6 (*RISM* 1553[24]). Phalèse's set of chanson books *a 4* was reissued in nearly identical volumes in 1554. Book 1 *a 4* no longer exists in its 1552 edition but only in the 1554 edition (*RISM* 1554[22]).

15. *RISM* 1553[5].

16. Winchester College, Fellows Library, MS. 153.

17. A modern facsimile of *Symphonia angelica* is available as vol. 21 of the Corpus of Early Music in Facsimile, ed. B.

Huys (Brussels: Editions culture et civilization, 1970). A second edition of *Symphonia angelica* was printed in 1590, and reprints were issued in 1594, 1611, and 1629. According to Fétis, *Biographie universelle* 8:392, collections with this title were published in 1565 by Scotto in Venice and by Waelrant and Laet in Antwerp. Cf. Weaver, "The Motets" 2:56–59, and Piel, *Studien zum Leben und Schaffen*, 66–67.

18. "Vorria morire" *a 4* had been printed, along with a version for four lutes, with a Flemish text, "Als ik u vinde," in Adriaenssen's *Pratum Musicum* the year before (see n. 5 above).

19. Slenk, "The Huguenot Psalter," 39.

20. Lowinsky, *Secret Chromatic Art*, 122ff. Lowinsky acknowledged (p. 126) that the themes were common to Calvinists and also those who were sympathetic to the new ideas but remained in the Catholic church. See also Weaver, "The Motets," vol. 1, chaps. 3–7. Lowinsky's thesis, which was received with some skepticism from the start, holds that a secret chromatic art existed among certain Netherlandish composers of the mid-sixteenth century, particularly Clemens non Papa and Waelrant, an art involving extended applications of musica ficta that carry the singers far afield harmonically and back again. As the full title of his book indicates (see n. 1), it is in the sacred motets that Lowinsky finds evidence for his hypothesis. Since he based his argument not only on the music itself but also on the texts, in which he saw evidence of Protestant theological emphases, the argument as formulated there would not apply to the present collection of secular music. In any case I have found no passages that seemed to require the addition of extended ficta. For a recent and thorough refutation of Lowinsky's theory that "chain reaction" ficta was normal sixteenth-century practice, see Karol Berger, "*Musica ficta*": *Theories of Accidental Inflections in Vocal Polyphony from Marchetto da Padova to Gioseffo Zarlino* (Cambridge: Cambridge University Press, 1987), esp. 89–90.

21. Fétis, *Biographie universelle* 8:392, lists a *Madrigali e canzoni francezi a 5* published by Susato in 1558. It is unlikely, however, that this volume ever existed. Cf. Ute Meissner, *Der antwerpener Notendrucker Tielman Susato* (Berlin: Merseburger, 1967), 2:131–32. See also Weaver, "The Motets," vol. 2, no. 30.

22. Waelrant divides six of the seven Italian sonnets between his two *parti* in the customary manner, an *ottava* and a *sestina*. Petrarch's "Volo con l'ali," however, is split inexplicably after the seventh line. This is clearly incorrect and raises the question of whether the composer understood the sense and syntax of the original.

23. *D'Orlando di Lassus il primo libro dovesi contengono madrigali, vilanesche, canzoni francesi, e motetti a quattro voci* (Antwerp: Susato, 1555). On the publication history of this volume, see Kristine K. Forney, "Orlando di Lasso's 'Opus 1': The Making and Marketing of a Renaissance Music Book," *Revue belge de musicologie* 39 (1985): 33–60. Forney provides a listing of the contents of Lassus's volume in her table 1.

24. The volumes by Cornet, Faignient, and Castro were all published by Jan de Laet, apparently without Waelrant's involvement. As noted above, Waelrant and Laet's last collaborative effort was the 1558 volume. The first four of Phalèse and Bellère's anthologies, *Musica divina* (1583), *Harmonia celeste* (1583), *Symphonia angelica* (1585), and *Melodia olympica* (1591), were popular well into the seventeenth century, as evidenced by reprintings and new editions as late as the 1640s. Besides Waelrant, Cornet, Faignient, and Castro, Netherlanders who composed madrigals included Schuyt, C. Verdonck, Pevernage, and Sweelinck. Cornet, in addition to the *canzoni napolitane* mentioned above, wrote

an entire volume of madrigals that was published by Christophe Plantin in 1581. Cf. G. van Doorslaer, "Severin Cornet—compositeur, maître de chapelle," in *De gulden passer*, new ser., vol. 3 (Antwerp: E. de Coker, 1925), 18–22.

25. Al Molto Mag.ᶜᵒ M. Bartholomeo Doria Inurea Vedendoui (Honoratissimo Signor mio) tra molte belle et nobilissime Parte, che come chiare stelle Risplendono In voi, a la Musica da un tempo in qua molto dedito, a l'armonia della quale, per Intervallo delle vostre cottidiane & honorate faccende, Solete il piu delle volte con gioiosissima conversatione ragunarui, Non ho trovata cosa la quale piu si convenga, a questa vostra virtuosa, & honesta delettatione, & al usitio, d'amorevole, & grato maestro: che presentarui una parte di quelle mie compositioni, ne le quali soglio tal volta piu tosto per mio passatempo e sodisfation, di molti miei maggiori, & Signori (tra quali voi sete il primo) che per alcuno altro rispetto eser citarmi: giudicando che per amar voi ardentemente questa faculta della Musica, & per esser cio che io vi dedico fatica, & parto mio no solo debba esser con lieto animo gradito & raccolto da voi ma anchora che sotto l'ombra del nome & valor vostro sia per rimaner coperto & difeso, contro a qual si voglia malignia oppositione certo & sicuro che appo voi verra di quei bei vestimenti ornato [(]il qual non gli ha potuto la poverta del mio ingegnio concedere) acceterete adunque questo mio debile & picol dono, come per arra de quel molto che io vi debbo & che merita il vostro valore, non lasciando d'amarmi & havermi in vostra protectione, aspettando da me quando da'l sommo iddio mi fia concesso, pegnio anchor piu chiaro & maggiore de l'affetione & oservanza mia verso di voi: iddio vi dia lunga & felice vita. D.V.S.S.

Huberto Waelrant.

26. The numbers used here to refer to pieces in the volume are not found in the source but are assigned here by the editor according to the order in which they appear in the source. Pieces of two parts are assigned a single number.

27. On the question of modal identification and tonal types in sixteenth-century music, see Harold Powers, "Tonal Types and Modal Categories," *Journal of the American Musicological Society* 34 (1981): 428–70, and idem, "Modal Representation in Polyphonic Offertories," *Early Music History: Studies in Medieval and Modern Music*, ed. Iain Fenlon, vol. 2 (Cambridge: Cambridge University Press, 1982), 43–86.

Modal designations here are based on the finals, the species of fifths and fourths used melodically, tones of prominent cadences, and the ambitus of the tenor. As is typical in music of this period, if the tenor spans the authentic range, so usually does the superius; altus and bassus then fall in the plagal range. If the tenor and superius use the plagal ambitus, the altus and bassus are authentic. In this volume the quintus usually has the same range as the tenor.

The second group of pieces with F as final, nos. 16–18, have tenors with a range covering both the authentic and the plagal ambitus, c–f′. The determination that these pieces are in the plagal mode, mode 6, therefore, depends on comparison with the range of the tenors of the first group of F pieces, nos. 4–6, which is f–a′. Other voices in the earlier group are similarly higher in pitch.

The mode of the pieces with C as final, no. 10 and nos. 19–20, is somewhat ambiguous. Number 10 could be assigned to mode 5 and nos. 19–20 to mode 6—in both cases, of course, in the commonly used transposition of that mode. Yet the emphasis on the lowered seventh degree in all three pieces (B-flat) suggests mode 7 or 8. At the same time, the prominence of E-flat and triads built on E-flat in several of the F pieces suggests that the lowered seventh is not foreign to Waelrant's use of modes 5 and 6 (cf. no. 17 or no. 5). Moreover, the final cadence of no. 10 (chord succession: a–F–c triads) would be less foreign to the G modes, which usually emphasize the fourth degree, than to the F modes, which almost invariably conclude with a clear V–I cadence. The same could be said regarding the final cadence of no. 19, which has the chord succession G–c–F–C. The *supplementum* after the final authentic cadence is more common to G modes than F modes. For these reasons I have chosen to assign no. 10 to mode 7 and nos. 19–20 to mode 8.

This method of identifying modes follows sixteenth-century theoretical discussions of the problem. Whether Waelrant as a composer ever thought in terms of mode as a precompositional concept cannot, of course, be known.

28. I am grateful to Timothy McTaggart, who is working on a dissertation on the *Jardin musical* series, for providing listings of the contents of the volumes by tonal type.

29. G. Becker, *Hubert Waelrant et ses psaumes* (Paris: Sandoz and Fischbacher, 1881), was not aware of this psalm setting. He describes only the eight in the *Jardin musical* series.

30. Although I am not sure if he was the first to employ the Marguerite wordplay, Clément Marot was the first to exploit it. His reference was, of course, to Marguerite of Navarre. Whether the Marguerite idea was then appropriated by other poets for other ladies of the same name or merely became a poetic tradition in its own right, Marguerite poems and musical settings of them continued to appear until late in the century. "De tout mon coeur j'ayme la Marguerite" was also set by Lassus (à 5); cf. Orlando di Lassus, *Sämtliche Werke*, ed. A. Sandberger (Leipzig: Breitkopf & Härtel, 1894–1926), 14:33. Another poem, "La Belle Marguerite," which is very similar in flavor and content, was set twice by Clemens non Papa, à 5 and à 6 (cf. Jacobus Clemens non Papa, *Opera Omnia*, ed. K. Ph. Bernet-Kempers [Rome: American Institute of Musicology, 1951–76], 10:82 and 119) and once by André Pevernage à 6 (cf. André Pevernage, *The Complete Chansons*, ed. Gerald R. Hoekstra, Recent Researches in the Music of the Renaissance, vol. 64 [Madison: A-R Editions, Inc., 1983], 51).

31. The numbering of Marot's poems follows the early editions supervised by the poet himself: *L'Adolescence clementine* of 1532 and *Les Oeuvres* of 1538. See Texts and Translations. For editions of the Marot poems set by Waelrant, see C. A. Mayer's editions of *Clément Marot: Oeuvres lyriques* (London: University of London, Athlone Press, 1964), *Clément Marot: Oeuvres diverses: Rondeaux, ballades, chants royeaux, épitaphes, étrennes and sonnets* (London: University of London, Athlone Press, 1966), and *Clément Marot: Les Epigrammes* (London: University of London, Athlone Press, 1970).

32. Cf. J. E. Kane, ed., *François I^er: Oeuvres poétiques* (Geneva: Editions Slatkine, 1984), 38. This poem was attributed to St.-Gelais in the edition of that poet's works (see Prosper Blanchemain, ed., *Oeuvres complètes de Mellin de Sainct-Gelais*, 3 vols. [Paris: P. Daffils, 1873]), but authorship by François I is confirmed by Kane on the basis of manuscript studies.

33. Cf. Wolfgang Boetticher, *Orlando di Lasso und seine Zeit, 1532–1594* (Kassel: Bärenreiter, 1958), 110, 113. Boetticher claims that the poem comes from *Traictez singuliers*

contenus au présent opusculle (Paris, 1525), which does contain a number of poems by Crétin as well as a "De tout mon coeur humblement je te salue," which must have been the source of Boetticher's confusion. Cf. Fréderic Lachèvre, *Bibliographie des recueils collectifs de poésies du XVIᵉ siècle* (Paris: Edouard Champion, 1922). The poem "De tout mon coeur j'ayme la Marguerite" does not appear in the 1932 edition of the poet's works either. Cf. Guillaume Crétin, *Oeuvres poétiques*, ed. Kathleen Chesney (Paris: Firmin-Didot, 1932).

34. See Brian Jeffery, *Chanson Verse of the Early Renaissance*, vol. 1 (London: B. Jeffery, 1971), 86–88, and vol. 2 (London: Tecla Editions, 1976), 289.

35. Cf. Lachèvre, *Bibliographie des recueils collectifs*. "Si je maintiens" has been ascribed to Saint-Gelais by Blanchemain, *Oeuvres complètes de Mellin de Sainct-Gelais* 3:8, but this is probably incorrect. The "Rochethulon" manuscript used by Blanchemain can no longer be found, but Ph. A. Becker, *Mellin de Saint Gelais: Eine kritische Studie* (Vienna: Hölder-Pichler-Tempsky, 1924), determined that this manuscript is not a collection of works by Saint-Gelais (Becker's conclusion is cited in Kane, *François Iᵉʳ*, 35 n. 76).

36. The five set by Waelrant are included in *Petrarch's Lyric Poems: The* Rime sparse *and Other Lyrics*, trans. and ed. Robert M. Durling (Cambridge, Mass.: Harvard University Press, 1976). The numbering of the poems is based on the order in which the poems appear in the final version of the *Rime sparse*, compiled by the poet himself and completed in 1374, on which Durling based his edition.

37. Cf. the passage translated in E. H. Wilkins, *Life of Petrarch* (Chicago: University of Chicago Press, 1961), 77.

38. Durling, *Petrarch's Lyric Poems*, 21.

39. For Petrarch, there was hardly an orthographic distinction between *Laura* and *l'aura*, since the apostrophe was not yet used in elisions.

40. Cf. Emil Vögel, Alfred Einstein, François Lesure, and Claudio Sartori, *Bibliografia della musica italiana vocale profana pubblicata dal 1500 al 1700* ["the new Vogel"] (Pomezia: Staderini, 1977), 1845–46.

41. Cf. Edward Williamson, *Bernardo Tasso* (Rome: Edizioni storia e letteratura, 1951), 46–49, and Alfred Einstein, *The Italian Madrigal* (Princeton, N.J.: Princeton University Press, 1949), 2:493–94.

42. Lassus left Rome for the Low Countries late spring 1554 in order to visit his parents, who were in poor health. When he arrived, however, he found that they had already died. He is known to have been in Antwerp in early 1555, and, in fact, he probably arrived as early as September of 1554. Presumably he left in 1556 when he accepted an appointment at the court of Albrecht V in Munich, but whether he spent all of this time in Antwerp has not been determined. Cf. Forney, "Orlando di Lasso's 'Opus 1,'" esp. 33, 37, and *The New Grove Dictionary of Music and Musicians*, s.v. "Lassus," by James Haar.

43. For example, in no. 8, "Fortunato colui," *seconda parte*, m. 13, the superius has "selu' o' n," the contratenor "selu' on," and the quinta "selu' ou."

44. For a guide to pronunciation of the early French, the more problematical of the two languages, the reader is referred to Jeannine Alton and Brian Jeffery, *Bele Buche e Bele Parleure: A Guide to the Pronunciation of Medieval and Renaissance French for Singers and Others* (London: Tecla Editions, 1976). A good historical overview of French pronunciation is E.-J. Bourciez, *Phonétique française* (Paris: Editions Klinckfieck, 19067).

# Texts and Translations

Translations of the French texts were made by the editor, who profited from the advice and assistance of Professor Cathy Yandell of the Carleton College Department of Romance Languages. The translations of the Petrarch sonnets are drawn from *Petrarch's Lyric Poems: The* Rime sparse *and Other Lyrics*, translated and edited by Robert M. Durling (Cambridge, Mass.: Harvard University Press, 1976). They are reprinted here with permission of the author and publisher. Translations of the four remaining madrigal texts were provided by Professor Charles Messner, also of the Carleton College Department of Romance Languages.

## [1]

E mi par d'hor in hor' udir' il messo
Che ma donna mi mand'a se chiamando;
Cosi dentr' e di fuor mi vo cangiando,
E son'in non molt'anni si dimesso
Ch'a pena riconosc' homai mi stesso:
Tutto 'l viver usat' ho mess'in bando.
Sarei contento di saper' il quando,
Ma pur devrebbe 'l temp'esser da presso.

I seem at every moment to hear the messenger
whom my lady sends calling to her;
thus within and without I go changing,
and in just a few years I have been so reduced
that by now I hardly recognize myself;
I have banished all my accustomed life.
I would be glad to know when,
but still the time ought to be near.

*Seconda parte*
O felice quel di che del terreno
Carcer' uscendo, lasci rott' e sparta
Questa mia grav' e fral' e mortal gonna
E da si folte tenebre mi parta,
Volando tanto su nel bel sereno
Ch'i' veggia 'l mio signore e la mia donna.

Oh happy that day when, going forth from my
earthly prison, I may leave broken and scattered
this heavy, frail, and mortal garment of mine,
and may depart from such thick shadows,
flying so far up into the beautiful sky
that I may see my Lord and my lady!

TEXT: Petrarch, *Rime sparse*, no. 349

## [2]

Moys amoureux, moys vestu de verdure,
Moys qui tant bien les coeurs fais esjouir,
Comment pourras veu l'ennuy que j'endure,
Faire le mien de liesse jouir?
Ne pres ne champs ne rossignolz ouir
N'y ont povoir: quoy donc? je te diray;
Fais seulement m'amie resjouir,
Incontinent je me resjouiray.

Amorous month, month clothed with verdure,
month, you make hearts delight so much,
how could you, seeing the weariness that I endure,
make my heart happy?
Neither meadows nor fields nor the nightingale
has the power to hear me: What then? I will tell you:
Only make my love happy,
forthwith I will rejoice.

TEXT: Clément Marot, Epigramme 147
NOTE ON THE TEXT: Line 7, Marot's original reads, "Tant seullement fayz Anne resjouyr." Marot's title is "Du moys de May et de Anne." Otherwise Waelrant's version follows the text as it appeared originally in Marot's *Oeuvres* (Lyon, 1538). Cf. C. A. Mayer, ed. *Clément Marot: Les Epigrammes* (London, University of London, Athlone Press, 1970), 209.

**[3]**

Sento l'aura mi' antica, e i dolci colli
Veggi' apparir' onde 'l bel lume nacque
Che tenne gli occhi miei, mentr'al Ciel piacque,
Bramos' e lieti, hor li tien trist' e molli.

O caduche speranze, o pensier folli!
Vedove l'herb' e torbide son l'acque
Et vot' e fredd'il nid'in ch'ella giacque,
Nel qual io viv' e morto giacer volli.

*Seconda parte*
Sperand' alfin da le soavi piante
E da' begli occhi suoi, che 'l cor m'hann' arso,
Ripos' alcun de le fatiche tante.
Ho servit' a signor crudel' e scarso:
Ch'arsi quant'il mio foco hebbi davante,
Hor vo piangend' il suo cenere sparso.

I feel the old breeze, and I see appearing
the sweet hills where the light was born
that kept my eyes full of desire and gladness,
while it pleased Heaven, and now keeps them sad
   and wet.
Oh short-lived hopes, oh mad cares!
The grass is bereaved and the waters troubled,
and empty and cold is the nest where she lay,
where I have wished to lie living and dead,

hoping to have from her gentle footprints
and her lovely glance, which so burned my heart,
some repose from my many labors.
I have served a cruel and niggardly lord:
I burned as long as my fire was before me,
now I go bewailing the scattering of its ashes.

TEXT: Petrarch, *Rime sparse*, no. 320

**[4]**

Une pastorelle gentille
Et un bergier en un vergier
L'autrier en jouant a la bille
S'entredisoyent, pour abreger,
   Roger
   Bergier,
   Legiere
   Bergiere,
C'est trop a la bille joué:
Chantons noé, noé, noé.

*Seconde partie*
Te souvient il plus du prophete
Qui nous dit un cas de hault faict,
Que d'une pucelle parfaicte
N'aistroit un enfant tout parfaict,
   L'effect
   Est faict:
   La belle
   Pucelle
A un filz du ciel advoué:
Chantons noé, noé, noé.

A pretty shepherdess
and a shepherd in an orchard
the other day, while playing a game,
said to each other—in short—
   "Shepherd
   Roger,"
   "Nimble
   shepherdess,"
"Enough of playing our game:
Let us sing, 'Noel, noel, noel.' "

Do you remember better the prophet
who tells us of such an important event
than you do a perfect maiden
who would bear a perfect child?
   It is
   a fact.
   The pretty
   Virgin
has a son approved by heaven:
Let us sing, "Noel, noel, noel."

TEXT: Clément Marot, Chanson 25
NOTE ON THE TEXT: *Seconde partie*, line 9: an earlier version of this line reads, "A
   eu ung filz au ciel voué." Cf. C. A. Meyer, ed., *Clément Marot: Oeuvres lyriques*
   (London: University of London, Athlone Press, 1964), 195; based on the 1530
   version published in Pierre Attaignant's *Trente et huyt chansons musicales*.
   Waelrant's text is based on the version that appeared in *L'Adolescence clementine* (1532).

## [5]

Amor piangev' e io con luy tal volta,
Dal qual miei passi non fur mai lontani,
Mirando per gl'effett' acerb' e strani
L'anima vostra de' suoi nodi sciolta;
Hor ch'al dritto camin l'ha Dio rivolta,
Col cor levand' al ciel'ambe le mani
Ringratio luy che' giusti pregh'humani
Benignamente sua merced' ascolta.

*Seconda parte*
E se tornand' a l'amorosa vita
Per farv'al bel desio volger le spalle
Trovaste per la via fossat' o poggi,
Fu per mostrar quant' e spinoso calle
E quant'alpestr' e dura la salita
Ond'al vero valor convien ch'uom poggi.

TEXT: Petrarch, *Rime sparse*, no. 25

Love, from whom my steps have never strayed,
used to weep, and I with him at times,
to see by the strange and bitter effects
that your soul was freed from his knots;
now that God has turned it back to the right path,
in my heart lifting both hands to heaven
I thank him who in his mercy
listens kindly to just human prayers.

And if, returning to the life of love,
you have found in your way ditches or hills
that try to make you abandon your lovely desire,
it was to show how thorny the path is,
how mountainous and hard the ascent
by which one must rise to true worth.

## [6]

Ogni giorno mi par più di mill'anni
Ch'i' segua la mia fid' e cara duce
Che mi conduss' al mondo hor mi conduce
Per miglior vi' a vita senz'affanni;
E non mi posson ritener gl'inganni
Del mondo, ch'i' l' conosc' e tanta luce
Dentr'al mio cor' infin dal ciel traluce
Ch'i' 'ncominci' a contar il temp' e i danni.

*Seconda parte*
Ne minaccie temer debbo di morte,
Che 'l Re sofferse con più grave pena
Per farm'a seguitar constant' e forte,

Et hor novellament' in ogni vena
Intro di lei che m'era dat'in sorte,
E non turbo la sua fronte serena.

TEXT: Petrarch, *Rime sparse*, no. 357

Every day seems to me more than a thousand years,
until I may follow my faithful, dear guide
who led me in the world and now leads me
by a better way to a life without troubles;
and the deceits of the world cannot hold me back,
for I know them, and so much light shines
within my heart all the way from heaven
that I begin to count up the time and my losses.

Nor do I fear the threats of death,
which the King suffered with worse pain
in order to make me constant and strong in following
      him.
and which recently entered each vein
of her who was allotted to me,
and did not cloud her clear brow.

## [7]

Dictes ouy ma dame ma maistresse,
Pour soustenir ma languissante vie
Jusques au jour propice a mon envie;
Puis, s'il vous plaist, faillez moy de promesse.
J'ayme trop mieux servir une maistresse
Disant ouy, plain de vaine esperance,
Que de tumber en facheuse tristesse
Par un nennyn voy fin de jouissance.

TEXT: François I.

Say yes, my lady and my mistress,
in order to sustain my languishing life
to the day favorable to my desire;
then, if it pleases you, fail me in the promise.
I much prefer, though full of vain hope,
to love a mistress who says yes,
than to fall into distressing sorrow
seeing the end of happiness with a no.

## [8]

Questa fera gentil che scherz' e fugge
Sul verd' e vag'april de' suo' begl'anni
E con leggiadr' et amoros' inganni
I cuor' altrui si dolcemente fugge,
Tigre non è, non l'animal che rugge,
O d'altra fer' acces' a nostri danni,
Ma tal che par che studi' ell' e s'affanni
Di dars'in preda a chi per lei si strugge.

*Seconda parte*
Fortunato colui che le bell'orme
Di lei seguendo la raggiung' al varco
In selv'o 'n riv'a un rio mentr'ella dorme;
Et ell'a lui di sudor moll' e carco
Desta, volgendo le celesti forme,
Lo scing' e di sua man gl'allenti l'arco.

This tender, wild creature that frolics and flees
across the pretty green April of her young years
and with charming and amorous wiles
so sweetly flees others' hearts
is not a tiger nor a roaring wild animal
or any other beast intent on harming us,
but, it would appear, of a kind that seeks and yearns
to become the prey of one who is consumed with
    desire for her.

Fortunate is the man who follows her beautiful tracks
and catches up with her at a clearing in the woods
or on the bank of a stream as she sleeps;
then she wakens and, turning her heavenly forms
toward his sweat-laden body,
ungirds him and with her hand releases his bow.

TEXT: A. F. Riccieri

## [9]

D'amours me va tout au rebours,
Ja ne fault que de cela mente,
J'ay refus en lieu de secours,
M'amie rit et je lamente;
C'est la cause pourquoy je chante:
D'amours me va tout au rebours.

In love everything goes contrary for me;
I must never lie about it.
I have refusal in place of succor,
my love laughs, and I weep;
that is the reason why I sing:
In love everything goes contrary for me.

TEXT: Clément Marot, Chanson 27
NOTE ON THE TEXT: In the version of this poem in Mayer's edition, *Clément Marot: Oeuvres lyriques*, 196, based on *L'Adolescence clementine* (Paris, 1532), there is an additional line at the end that reads, "Tout au rebours me va d'amours."

## [10]

Chius'er' il sol d'un tenebroso velo
Che si stendea fin a l'estreme sponde
Del orizonte e mormorar le fronde
S'udian' e tuon'andar scorrend' il cielo.
Di poggia in dubbio tempestoso gelo
Stav'io per gir' oltre le torbid' onde
Del fium'altier ch'il gran sepolcr' asconde
Del figli' audace del signor di Delo.

*Seconda parte*
Quand'apparir su l'altra rip'il lume
De' be' vostr'occhi vid' e udi parole
Che Leandro potean far mi quel giorno;

E tutt'a un temp'i nuvoli d'intorno
Si dileguar' e si scopers' il sole,
Tacquer' i venti e tranquillos' il fiume.

The sun was obscured by the shadowy veil,
which stretched up to the farthest shores
of the horizon, and one heard branches murmuring
and thunder running across the sky.
To leeward stood I in dubious, stormy cold
in order to turn beyond the troubled waves
of the proud river that hides the great sepulchre
of the bold son of the lord of Delos.

When on the other shore I saw
the light of your beautiful eyes appear
and heard words which that day had the power to
    make me a Leander,
then at once the clouds all around
faded away, and the sun appeared;
the winds calmed, and the river became quiet.

TEXT: Ludovico Ariosto

## [11]

Si je maintiens ma vie seulement
Par ton regard, qu'est ce que je feray?
Si tu le metz autre part je mouray,
Et toy bientost apres certainement;
Car lorsque mort finera mon tourment
Te sentiras sans forc' et sans valeur
Puisque vivons l'ung par l'autr' aysément,
Moy de ton oeil et toy de ma doleur.

If I am able to sustain my life
only through your eyes, what shall I do?
If you direct them elsewhere, I will die,
and you soon after, certainly;
for when death ends my torment
you will feel yourself without strength or worth,
since we live one off the other easily,
I from your glance, and you from my sorrow.

NOTE ON THE TEXT: Line 8: source has *ton dueil* for *ton oeil*.

## [12]

Ahi dispietat' amor come consenti
Ch'io meni vita si penos' e ria,
Solcand' un ampio mar d'aspri tormenti
Per cosi lung' e perigliosa via?
De perche fiato de benigni venti
Non so spinge la stanca nave mia,
Si che dop'un camin si lung' e torto
Possa chiuder la vel'in questo porto?

Ah, pitiless love, how can you consent
that I should lead a life so painful and cruel,
ploughing a full sea of harsh torments
through such a long and perilous course?
Oh, why doesn't a breath of favorable winds,
for instance, drive my tired ship,
so that after so long and tortuous a road
I might lower my sails in this port?

*Seconda parte*
Ma scorga mi destin empi' e rapace
Dove l'orsa del ciel il mond'agghiaccia,
O dove Phebo con la calda face
Arde del bel terren la vaga faccia;
Che 'l nodo cosi strett' e si tenace,
Che 'l vostro col mio cor string' et allaccia,
Non fia mai chi ralenti, o chi discioglia,

Mentr'havra verde allor' e ram' e foglia.

But let my wicked, rapacious destiny perceive me
where the she-bear of heaven freezes the world,
or where Phoebus with his hot torch
burns the lovely face of earthly beauty;
for the knot is so tight and so unyielding
that squeezes and binds your heart with mine,
there will never be anyone who can loosen or
    untie it
as long as branches and leaves remain green.

TEXT: Bernardo Tasso
NOTE ON THE TEXT: *Seconda parte*, line 6: source reads *Che 'l nostro*; the 1560 edition
of Tasso's *Rime* reads *Che 'l vostro*.

## [13]

Souvent au joly moys de May
La terre mue et renouvelle
Maintz amoureux font ainsi gay,
Subjectz a faire amour nouvelle,
Par legiereté de cervelle,
Ou pour estr' ailleurs plus contens;
Ma façon d'aymer n'est pas telle:
Mes amours durent en tout temps.

Often in the merry month of May
the earth molts and renews,
and many lovers are likewise merry
and prone to making new love—
by lightness of head—
or to be more content with someone else.
My style of love is not such:
my loves last for all time.

TEXT: Clément Marot, Ballade 19
NOTE ON THE TEXT: Marot's poem "Chant de May et de vertu" begins, "Vo-
luntiers en ce moys ici / la terre mue et renouvelle / Maintz amoureux et font
ainsi / subjectz a faire amour nouvelle." This makes more sense grammatically
than the corrupted version in Waelrant's setting. Cf. *Clément Marot: Oeuvres
diverses. Rondeaux, ballades, chants royeaux, épitaphes, étrennes and sonnets*, ed.
C. A. Mayer (London: University of London, Athlone Press, 1966), Ballade
19. There follow two more strophes and an *envoi*.

**[14]**

Ferma speranz' e fe pur' e sincera,
Grave travagli' e afflitta gelosia,

Contien' il don'in se ch'a voi s'invia;
Ne fu mai cosa si valid' e vera,
E in me temp'alcun non fia che pera
L'impression' ch'il cuor tien'in balia;
Ferm' e per non cader la speme mia,
Ne men la fed' e patt'in giuso fera.

*Seconda parte*
Geloza spero e per mortell'i pero,
E la fe qual columb' e ogn'hor più salda;
E in quest'objetti ogn'hor morendo vivo,
Ne pero mai d'amor mi spogli' o privo;
E segno vi ne fa che 'l che mi scalda
L'azzurro, il verde, il bigio, il bianch' e 'l nero,
E fa il concett' intiero il vag' e bel morato

Che nel petto chiud' e tien stretto l'amor mio
    secreto.

The gift that is being sent to you
contains within itself firm hope, pure and sincere
    faith,
heavy torment, and afflicted jealousy.
There was never anything so valid and true,
and in me there will never be a time when shall perish
the impression that holds my heart in its power.
My hope is so strong that it will not fall
nor strike down my faith and pact.

Jealous, I hope and perish of anguish,
with faith like a dove's, ever more steadfast,
and in these purposes each hour dying, I live;
yet I never renounce or deprive myself of love;
a sign thereof to you is that what excites me
is blue, green, gray, white, and black;
and the conceit is made complete by the charming,
    handsome Moor
that my secret love encloses and holds tight in my
    breast.

**[15]**

Or suis je bien au pire
De mes malheureux jours,
Mon cas trop fort sempire,
Et me vient au rebours.
Et tout cela me font amours,
Dont j'endure si grief martire:
Si n'ay de vous autre secours,
Force sera que me retire.

Now am I truly in the worst
of my unfortunate days.
My situation, too heavy, grows worse,
and comes to me the wrong way.
And love, from which I endure such
great suffering, does all that to me.
If I do not have other succor from you,
I will not be able to do anything but give up.

**[16]**

Un jour passé bien escoutoye
Une fille secretement
En lieu secret demenant joye,
Qui triumphoit joyeusement,
Considerant qu'en mariage
Debvoit avoir son avantage,
Au joly jeu sans insolence,
Dont elle dit en sa langage,
Je suis gay, gay pour dimence.

One day a while ago
I secretly heard a girl
in a secret place making merry,
who exulted joyously,
considering that marriage
would be to her advantage,
rather than a carefree existence.
Concerning this she said in her own words,
"I am beside myself with joy."

NOTE ON THE TEXT: Line 8: instead of *sa langage* source has *son langage*.

**[17]**

Volo con l'ali di pensier' al cielo
Si spesse volte che quas'un di loro
Esser mi par ch'an iv'il suo thesoro,
Lasciand' in terra lo squarciato velo.
Tal hor mi trema 'l cor d'un dolce gielo,
Udendo lei per ch'io mi discoloro
Dirmi: amic' hor t'am' io e hor t'honoro.

I fly with the wings of thought to heaven so often
that it seems to me I am almost one of those
who there possess their treasure,
leaving on earth their rent veils.
Sometimes my heart trembles with a sweet chill,
hearing her for whom I grow pale say to me:
"Friend, now I love you and now I honor you,

*Seconda parte*
Per ch'a' i costumi variat' e 'l pelo.

Menam' al suo Signor; alhor m'inchino,
Pregand' humilemente che consenta
Ch'i' sti' a veder e l'un' e l'altro volto.
Risponde: Egl' e ben fermo il tuo destino,
E per tardar anchor vent'ann' o trenta
Parr'a te troppo, e non fia però molto.

because you have changed your habits and
        your hair."
She leads me to her Lord;
then I incline myself, humbly begging
that he permit me to stay to see their two faces.
He replies: "Your destiny is certain,
and a delay of twenty or thirty years
will seem much to you, but it will be little."

TEXT: Petrarch, *Rime sparse*, no. 362
NOTE ON THE TEXT: Waelrant clearly makes an error in dividing the poem after
the seventh line. Considering both the structure of the sonnet and the mean-
ing, the division should be after *pelo*.

## [18]

De tout mon coeur t'exalteray,
Seigneur, et si racompteray
Toutes tes oeuvres non pareilles,
Qui sont dignes de grands merveilles.

With all my heart will I exalt you,
Lord, and so will recount
all your marvelous works,
which are worthy of great wonder.

TEXT: Clément Marot, trans., Psalm 9, verse 1

## [19]

De tout mon coeur j'ayme la Marguerite,
Et dis pour vray combien qu'elle est petitte,
Qu'elle precèd' en bonté et valeur,
Beaulté, couleur, tout aultre playsant fleur,
Par quoy surtout qui vouldra s'en despite.
De tout mon coeur j'ayme la Marguerite.

With all my heart I love the daisy [Margaret]
and say truly that though she is small
yet she exceeds in kindness and worth,
beauty and color, every other pretty flower;
therefore, let whomever would, fret over it.
With all my heart I love the daisy.

## [20]

Soyons playsantz encore demiheure,
Laissons tout dueil, prennons nostre playsir.
Ainsi faysant le meilleur nous demeure;
En triumphant quant nous avons loysir.
Si nous gardons de tristess' encourir,
Car une fois c'est une chose seure,
Qu'un jour viendra qu'il nous fauldra morir:
Soyons playsantz encore demiheure.

Let us all make merry yet for half an hour,
let us leave all sorrow, let us take our pleasure.
Thus doing, the best remains for us,
by rejoicing when we have leisure.
So we guard against incurring sadness,
for one thing is certain,
that the day will come that we must die.
Let us all make merry yet for half an hour.

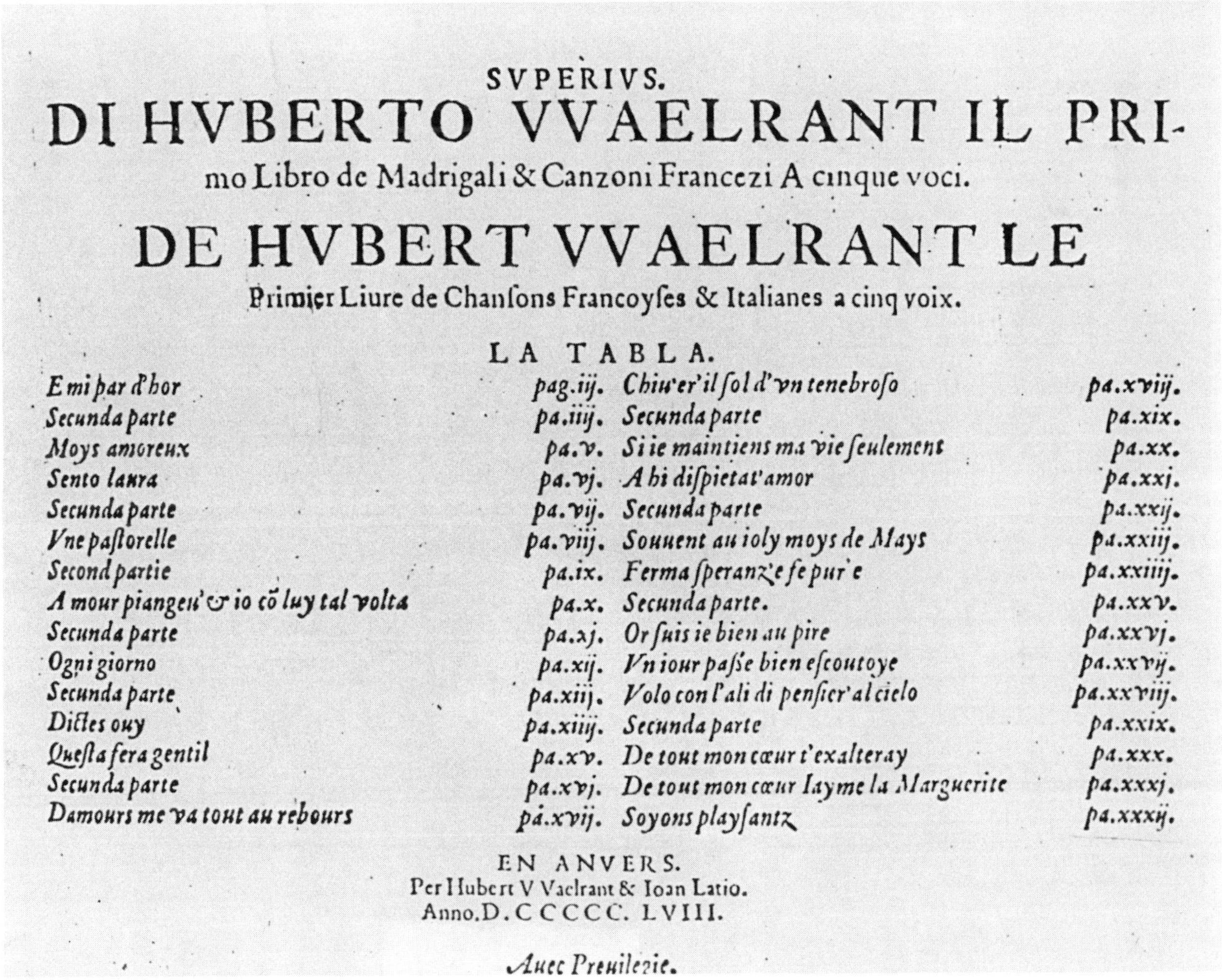

SVPERIVS.

# DI HVBERTO VVAELRANT IL PRI-

mo Libro de Madrigali & Canzoni Francezi A cinque voci.

# DE HVBERT VVAELRANT LE

Primier Liure de Chanſons Francoyſes & Italianes a cinq voix.

## LA TABLA.

EN ANVERS.
Per Hubert V Vaelrant & Ioan Latio.
Anno.D.CCCCC.LVIII.

Auec Preuilegie.

PLATE 1. Hubert Waelrant, *Il Primo Libro de Madrigali e Canzoni Francezi*. Title page from the superius partbook. (Courtesy Bayerische Staatsbibliothek, Munich)

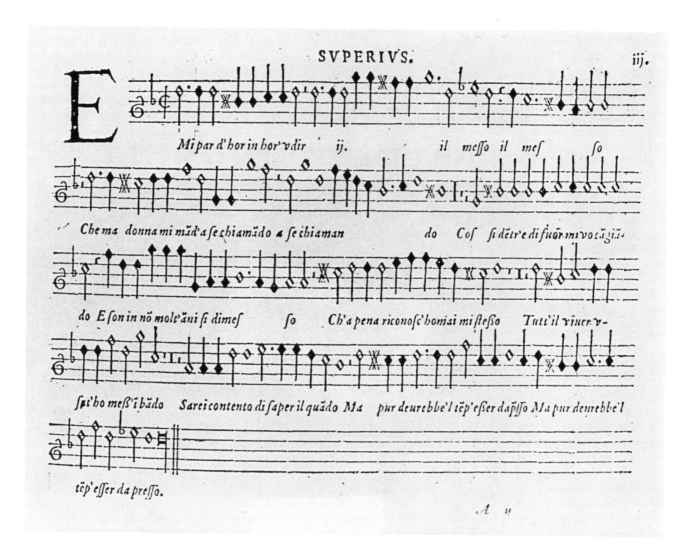

PLATE 2. Hubert Waelrant, *Il Primo Libro de Madrigali e Canzoni Francezi*. Music page from the superius partbook. (Courtesy Bayerische Staatsbibliothek, Munich)

# [1] E mi par d'hor in hor' udir' il messo

-do, E son' in non mol- t'an-ni si di- mes - so Ch'a pe- na ri-

-do, E son' in non ___ mol-t'an-ni si di- mes- so Ch'a pe- na ri-

-do,) E son' in non mol- t'an-ni si di-mes- so Ch'a pe- na ri-

-do, E son' in non mol- t'an- ni si di- mes- so Ch'a pe- na ri-

son' in non mol-t'an- ni si di- mes- so

- co- no- sc'ho-mai mi stes- so:

- co- no- sc'ho-mai mi stes- so, Ch'a pe- na ri- co- no- sc'ho-mai mi stes-

- co- no- sc'ho-mai mi stes- so, Ch'a pe- na ⟨ri- co- no- sc'ho-mai ni stes-

- co- no- sc'ho-mai mi stes- so, Ch'a pe- na ri- co- no- sc'ho-mai mi stes-

Ch'a pe- na ri- co- no- sc'ho-mai mi stes-

Tut- to'l vi- ver u- sa- t'ho mes- s'in ban- do.

- so: Tut- to'l vi- ver u- sa- t'ho mes- s'in ban- do,

- so:) Tut- to'l vi- ver u- sa-

-so: Tut- to'l vi- ver u- sa- t'ho mes- s'in ban- do, ho mes-

-so: Tut- to'l vi- ver u- sa- t'ho mes- s'in ban-

**Seconda parte**

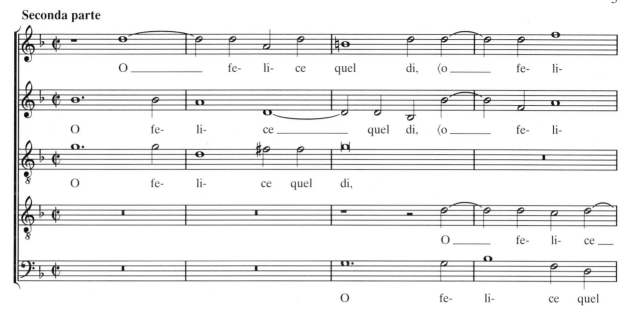

O _____ fe- li- ce quel di, ⟨o _____ fe- li-
O fe- li- ce _____ quel di, ⟨o _____ fe- li-
O fe- li- ce quel di,
O _____ fe- li- ce _____
O fe- li- ce quel

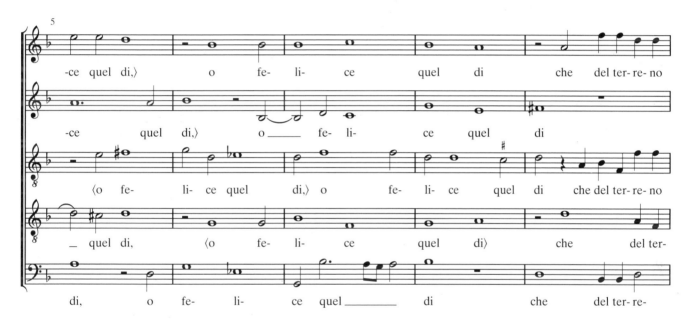

-ce quel di,⟩ o fe- li- ce quel di che del ter- re- no
-ce quel di,⟩ o _____ fe- li- ce quel di
⟨o fe- li- ce quel di,⟩ o fe- li- ce quel di che del ter- re- no
_ quel di, ⟨o fe- li- ce quel di⟩ che del ter-
di, o fe- li- ce quel _____ di che del ter- re-

Car- ce- r'u- scen- do, la- sci rot- t'e spar- ta, la- sci rot- t'e
che del ter- re- no Car- ce- r'u- scen- do, la- sci rot- t'e
Car- ce- r'u- scen- do, la- sci rot- t'e spar- ta
-re- no, ⟨che del ter- re- no⟩ Car- ce- r'u- scen- do, la- sci rot- t'e
-no, che del ter- re- no Car- ce- r'u- scen- do, la- sci rot- t'e

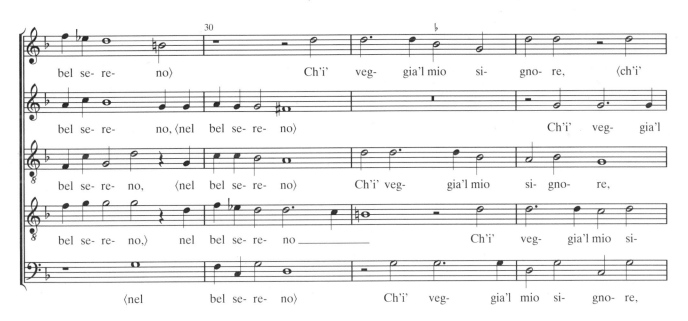

# [2] Moys amoureux, moys vestu de verdure

[Clément Marot]

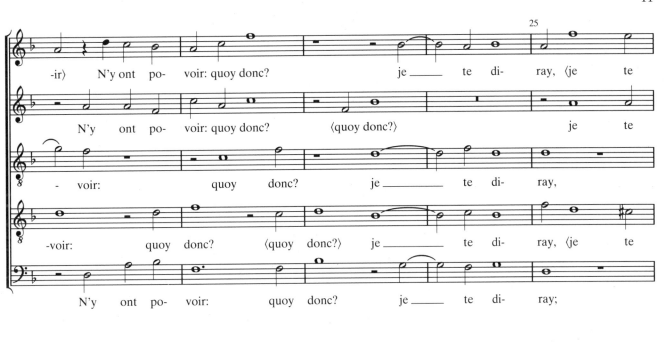

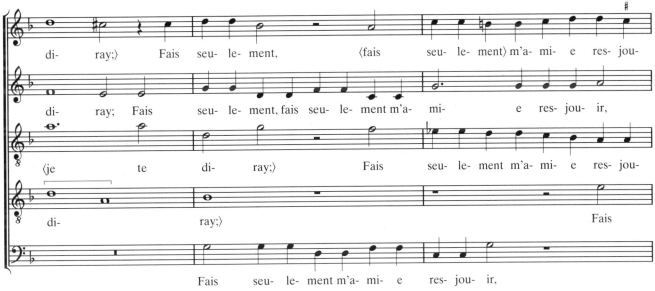

# [3] Sento l'aura mi' antica, e i dolci colli

**Seconda parte**

# [4] Une pastorelle gentille

[Clément Marot]

**Seconde partie**

24

# [5] Amor piangev' e io con luy tal volta

[Petrarch]

giu- sti pregh' hu- ma- ni   Be- ni- - gna- men-
-ni   Be- ni- gna- men- te sua mer- ce- d'a-
hu- ma- ni   Be- ni- - gna- men- te sua mer- ce- d'a-
_ hu- ma- ni   Be- ni- gna- men- te _
hu- ma- ni   Be- ni- - gna- men-

- te sua mer- ce- d'a- scol- ta.
-scol- ta, Be- ni- gna- men- te sua mer- ce- d'a- scol- ta.
-scol- ta, sua _ mer- ce- d'a- scol- ta.
_ sua mer- ce- d'a- scol- ta.
-te sua _ mer- ce- d'a- scol- ta.

**Seconda parte**

E se tor- nan- - d'a l'a- mo- ro- sa
E se tor- nan- d'a l'a- mo- ro- sa vi- ta,
E se tor- nan- d'a l'a- mo- ro- sa vi- ta,
E _ se tor- nan- d'a

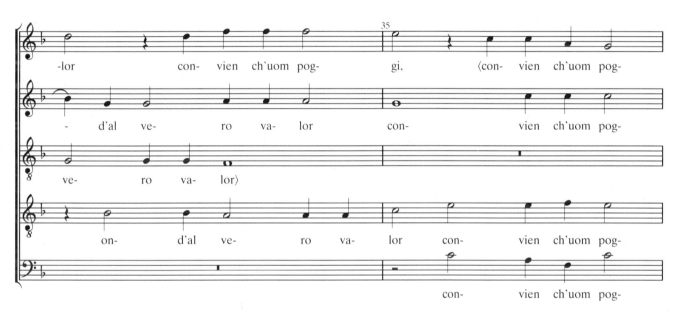

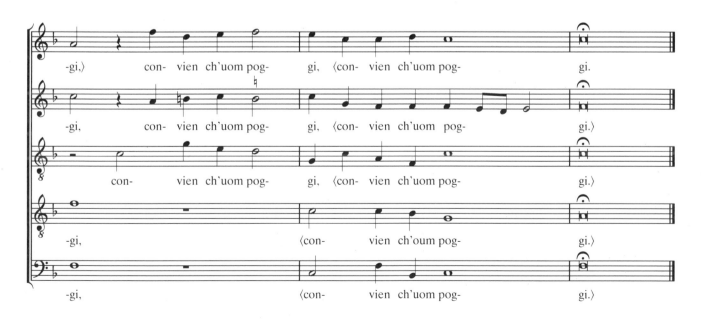

# [6] Ogni giorno mi par più di mill'anni

Petrarch

**Seconda parte**

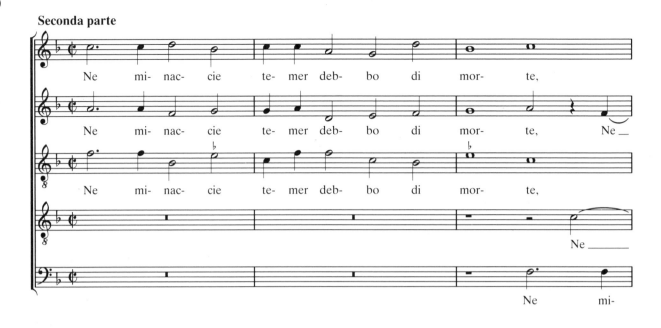

Ne mi- nac- cie te- mer deb- bo di mor- te,

Ne mi- nac- cie te- mer deb- bo di mor- te, Ne __

Ne mi- nac- cie te- mer deb- bo di mor- te,

Ne _____

Ne mi-

Ne mi- nac- cie te- mer deb- bo di mor- te, Che'l ____

__ mi- nac- cie te- mer deb- bo di mor- te, Che'l

Che'l Re sof-

__ mi- nac- cie te- mer deb- bo di mor- te,

-nac- cie te- mer deb- bo di mor- te, Che'l

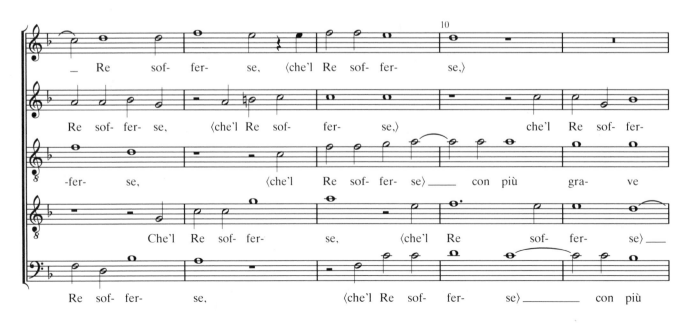

__ Re sof- fer- se, ⟨che'l Re sof- fer- se,⟩

Re sof- fer- se, ⟨che'l Re sof- fer- se,⟩ che'l Re sof- fer-

-fer- se, ⟨che'l Re sof- fer- se⟩ ____ con più gra- ve

Che'l Re sof- fer- se, ⟨che'l Re sof- fer- se⟩ ____

Re sof- fer- se, ⟨che'l Re sof- fer- se⟩ ____ con più

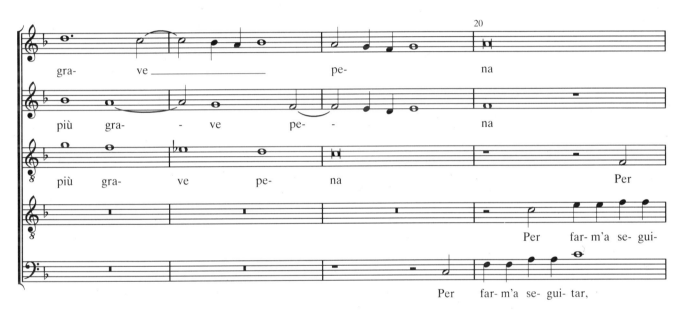

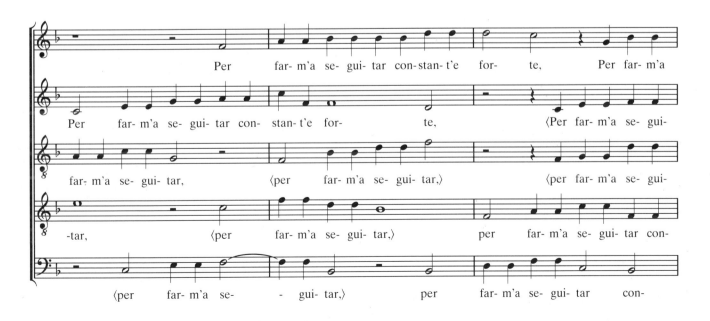

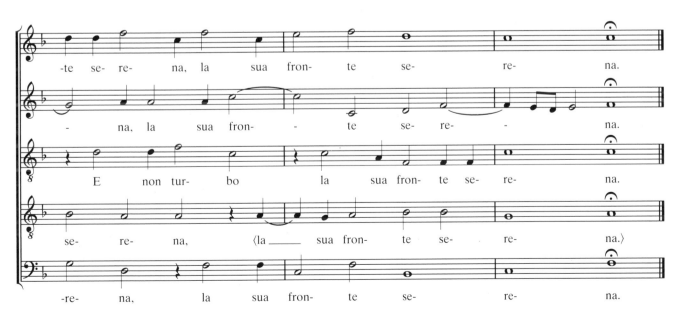

# [7] Dictes ouy ma dame ma maistresse

[François I]

# [8] Questa fera gentil che scherz' e fugge

[A. F. Riccieri]

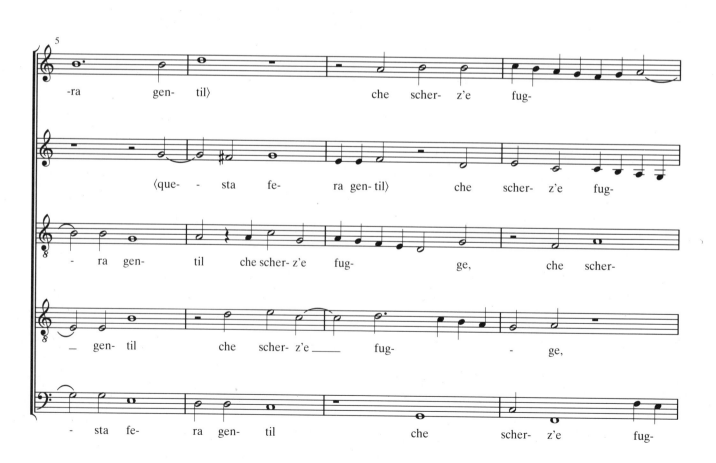

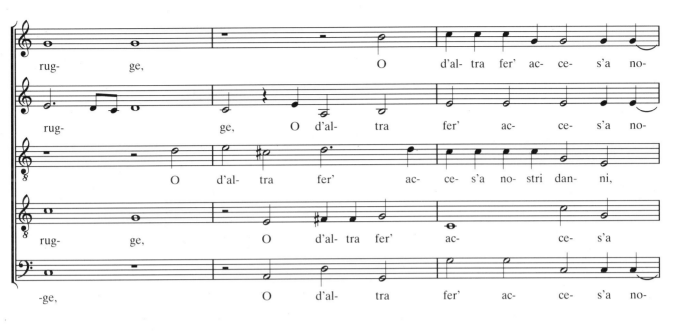

**Seconda parte**

54

# [9] D'amours me va tout au rebours

[Clément Marot]

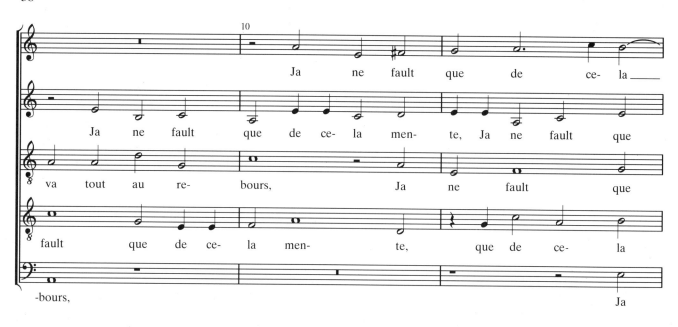

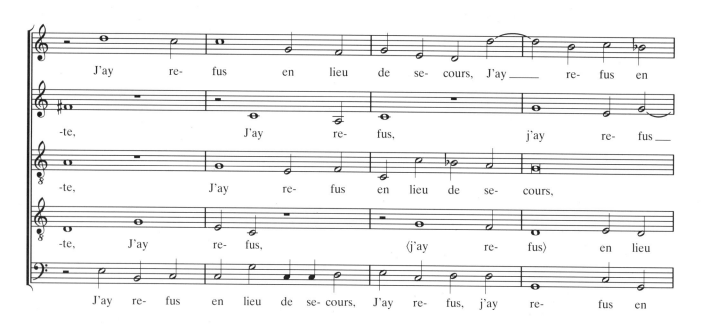

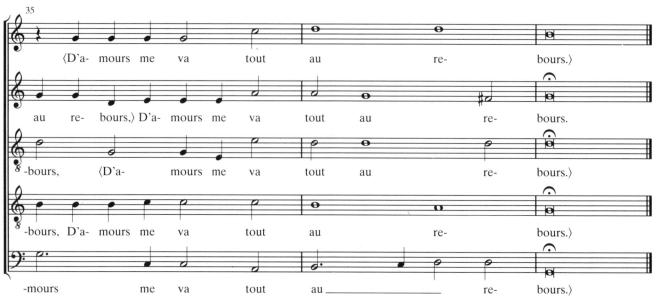

# [10] Chius'er' il sol d'un tenebroso velo

[Ludovico Ariosto]

a l'e- stre- me spon- de Del o- ri- zon- te e mor-mo- rar le
-me spon- de Del o- ri- zon- t'e mor-mo- rar le
fin a l'e- stre- me spon- de Del o- ri- zon- te e
-stre- me spon- de Del o- ri- zon- te
-stre- me spon- de Del o- ri- zon- te _____

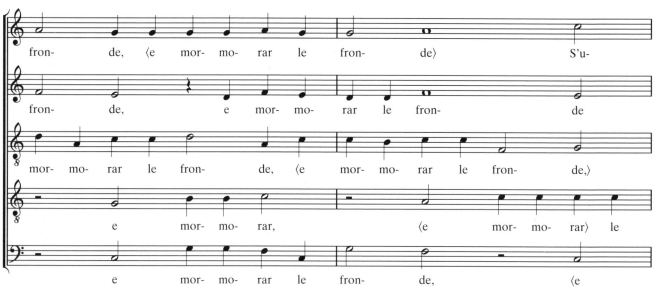

fron- de, ⟨e mor- mo- rar le fron- de⟩ S'u-
fron- de, e mor- mo- rar le fron- de
mor- mo- rar le fron- de, ⟨e mor- mo- rar le fron- de,⟩
e mor- mo- rar, ⟨e mor- mo- rar⟩ le
e mor- mo- rar le fron- de, ⟨e

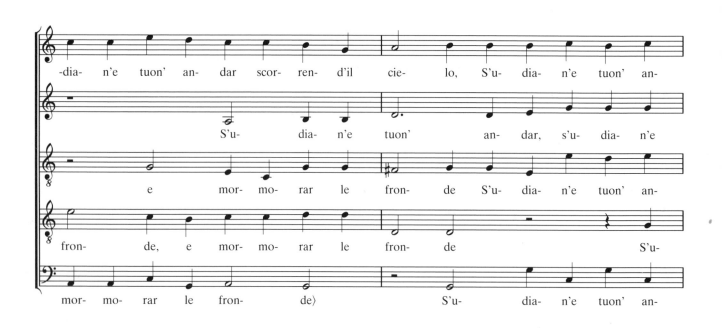

-dia- n'e tuon' an- dar scor- ren- d'il cie- lo, S'u- dia- n'e tuon' an-
S'u- dia- n'e tuon' an- dar, s'u- dia- n'e
e mor- mo- rar le fron- de S'u- dia- n'e tuon' an-
fron- de, e mor- mo- rar le fron- de S'u-
mor- mo- rar le fron- de⟩ S'u- dia- n'e tuon' an-

-ce) del si- gnor, del ____ si- gnor di De- lo.

De- lo, del ____ si- gnor ____ di De- lo.

De- lo, del si- gnor di De- lo, di De- lo.

⟨del fi- gli'au- da- ce⟩ del si- gnor di De- lo.

De- lo, del ____ si- gnor di De- lo.

**Seconda parte**

Quan- d'ap- pa- rir su l'al- tra

Quan- d'ap- pa- rir su l'al- tra ri- pa, su

Quan- d'ap- pa- rir su l'al- tra ____ rip' il

Quan- d'ap- -pa- rir su l'al- tra rip' ____ il lu-

Quan- d'ap- -pa- rir su l'al- tra rip' il lu-

rip' il lu- -me De' be' vo- str'oc- chi vid' e u-

l'al- tra rip' il lu- me De' be' vo- str'oc- chi vid' e u- di pa- ro-

lu- me, su l'al- tra rip' il ____ lu- me De' be' vo- str'oc- chi vid' e u-

-me De' be' vo- str'oc- chi vid' ____ e u- di pa- ro- le, vid' e u-

-me De' be' vo- str'oc- chi vid' e u- di ____ pa- ro-

Che Le- an- dro po- -tean far mi quel gior- -no;

Che Le- an- dro po- tean far mi quel gior- no, quel gior- no;

quel gior- no, ⟨Che Le- an- dro po- tean — far mi quel gior- no;⟩

-dro po- tean far mi quel gior- no, — far mi quel gior- no;

mi quel gior- no;

E tut- t'a un tem- p'i nu- vo- li d'in- tor- no Si di- le- -gua-r'e si sco- per-

E tut- t'a un tem- p'i nu- vo- li d'in- tor- no Si — di- le-gua-r'e

E tut- t'a un tem- p'i nu- vo- li- d'in- tor- no Si di- le-gua- r'e si sco-

E tut- t'a un tem- p'i nu- vo- li d'in- tor- no Si di- le- gua- r'e si sco-per-s'il so-

E tut- t'a un tem- p'i nu- vo- li d'in- tor- no Si di- le- gua- r'e

- s'il so- le, il so- le, Tac-

si sco- per- s'il so- le, Tac-

-per- s'il so- le, il so- le, Tac- que-r'i ven- ti,

-le, Tac- que-r'i ven- ti,

si sco- per- s'il so- le, Tac- que-r'i ven- ti,

68

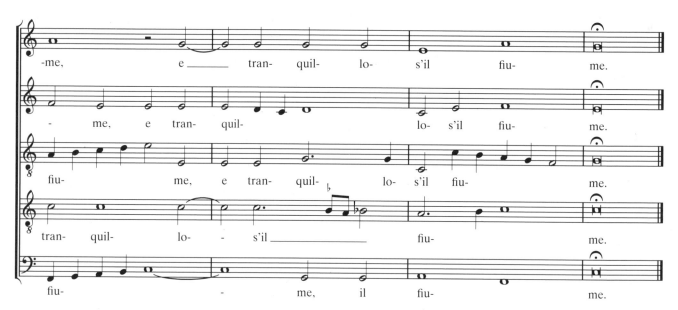

# [11] Si je maintiens ma vie seulement

Superius: Si je main- tiens ma vi- e seu- - le- ment,

Contratenor: Si je main- tiens ma vi- e seu- le- ment, _____ ma vi-

Quinta: Si je main- tiens ma vi- e seu- le- ment

Tenor: Si je main- tiens ma

Bassus: Si

⟨Si je main- tiens ma vi- e seu- - le- ment⟩

- e seu- le- ment Par ton re- gard, ⟨par ton _____ re-

Par ton re- gard, ⟨par ton re- gard,⟩ par

vi- e seu- le- ment Par ton re- gard,

je main- tiens ma vi- e seu- le- ment Par ton re-

# [12] Ahi dispietat' amor come consenti

[Bernardo Tasso]

**Seconda parte**

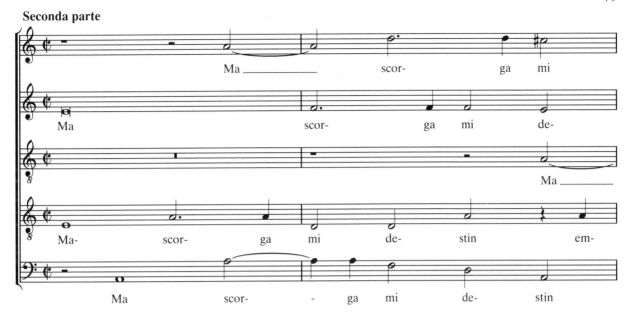

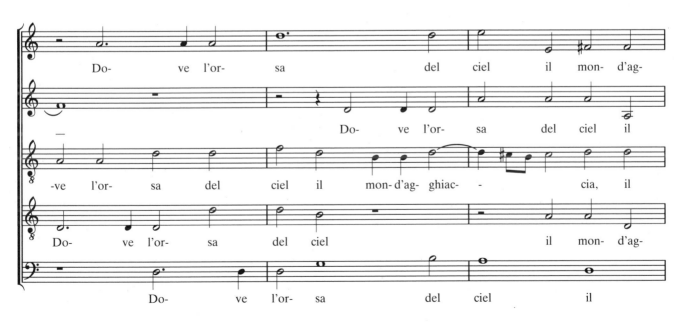

# [13] Souvent au joly moys de May

[Clément Marot]

# [14] Ferma speranz' e fe pur' e sincera

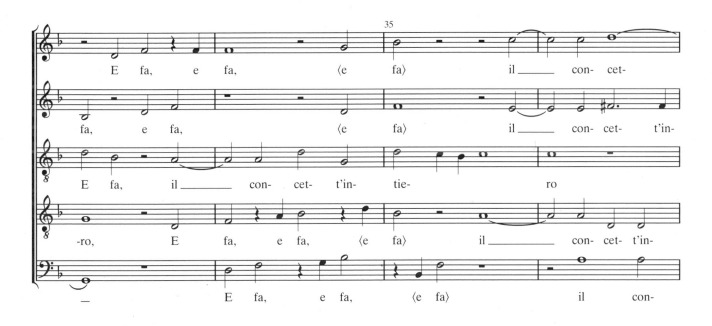

# [15] Or suis je bien au pire

# [16] Un jour passé bien escoutoye

# [17] Volo con l'ali di pensier' al cielo

[Petrarch]

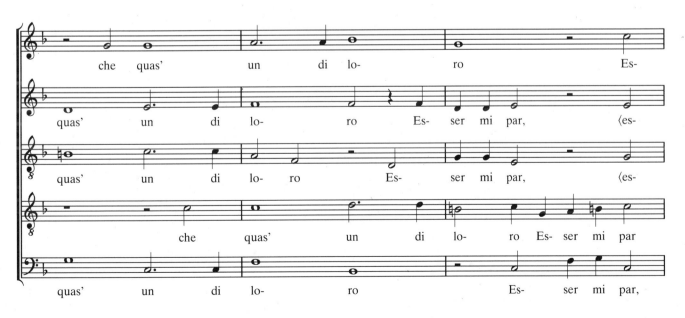

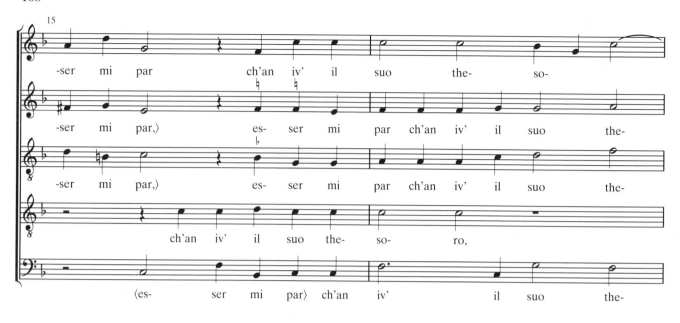

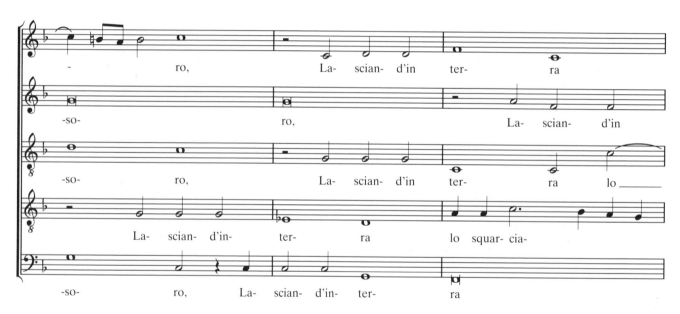

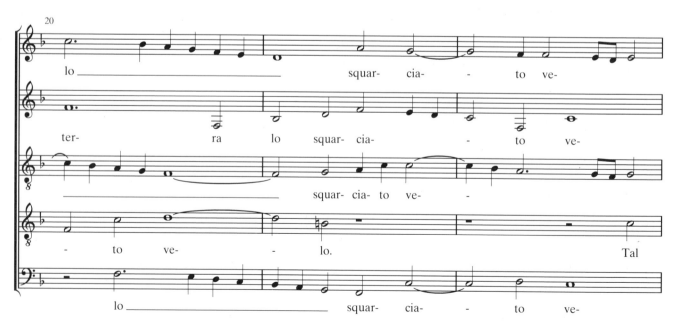

**Seconda parte**

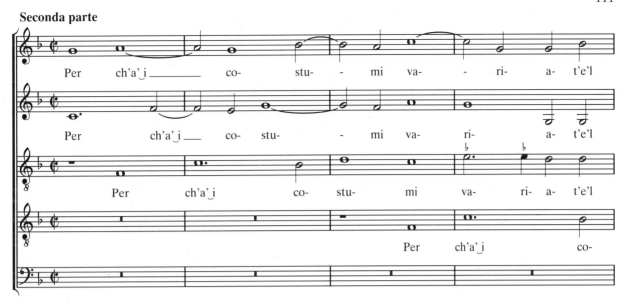

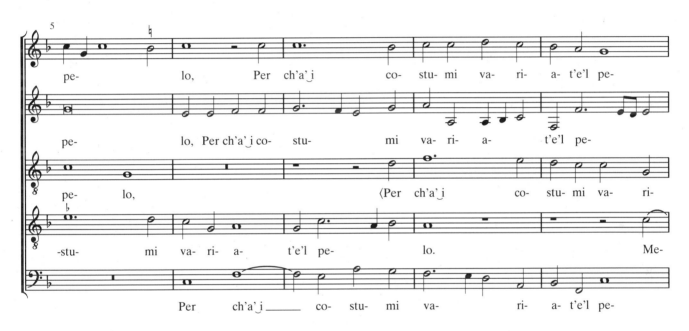

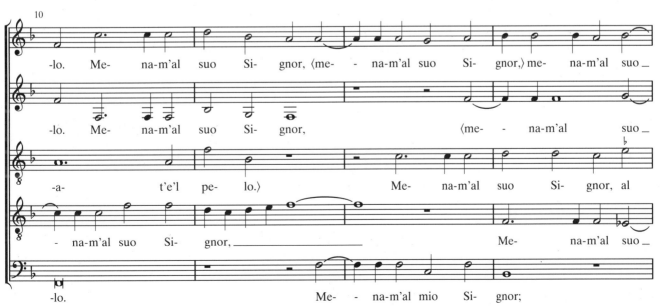

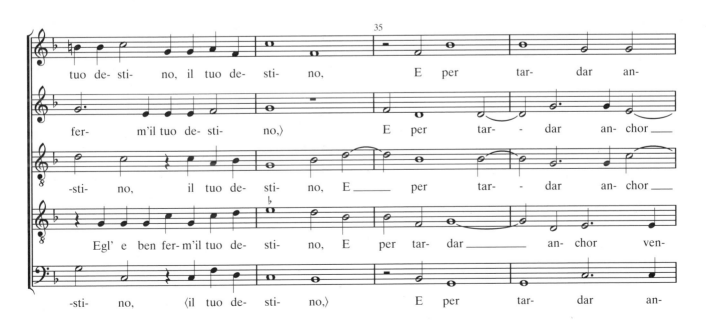

# [18] De tout mon coeur t'exalteray

[Clément Marot (Psalm 9)]

116

# [19] De tout mon coeur j'ayme la Marguerite

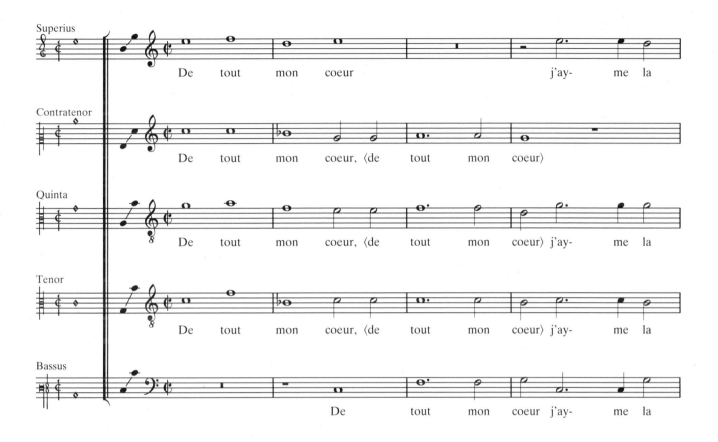

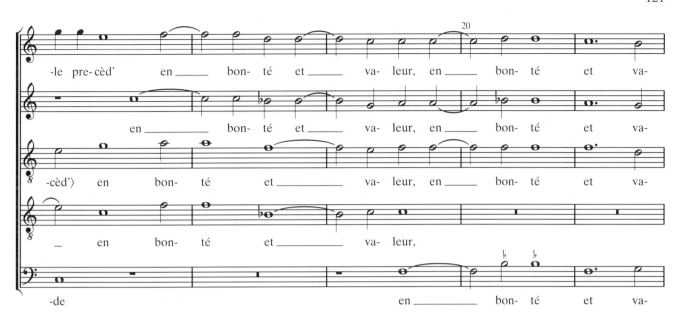

-le pre-cèd' en _____ bon- té et _____ va- leur, en _____ bon- té et va-

en _____ bon- té et _____ va- leur, en _____ bon- té et va-

-cèd') en bon- té et _____ va- leur, en _____ bon- té et va-

_ en bon- té et _____ va- leur,

-de en _____ bon- té et va-

-leur, Beaul- té, cou- leur, tout aul- tre play- sant fleur, ⟨Beaul- té, cou- leur, tout aul- tre

-leur, Beaul- té, cou- leur, tout aul- tre play- sant fleur, ⟨Beaul- té, cou- leur, tout aul- tre

-leur, Beaul- té, cou- leur, tout aul- tre play- sant fleur, ⟨Beaul- té, cou- leur, tout aul- tre

Beaul- tè, cou- leur, tout aul- tre play- sant fleur, ⟨Beaul- té, cou- leur, tout aul- tre

-leur, Beaul- té, cou- leur, tout aul- tre

play- sant fleur,⟩ Par quoy sur- tout qui voul- dra s'en des- pi- te, qui

play- sant fleur,⟩ Par quoy sur- tout qui voul- dra s'en des- pi- te, ⟨qui

play- sant fleur,⟩ Par quoy sur- tout qui voul- dra s'en des- pi- te, qui

play- sant fleur,⟩ Par quoy sur- tout qui

play- sant fleur, Par quoy sur- tout qui voul- dra s'en des- pi- te.

# [20] Soyons playsantz encore demiheure

124

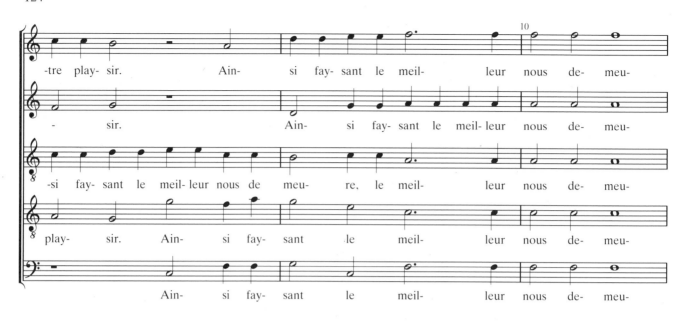

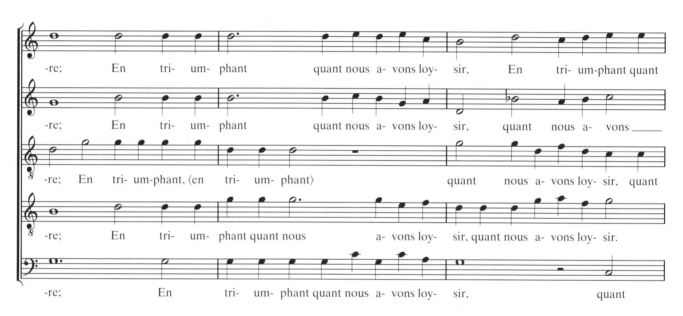